"You're seri
"Someone's
you want m
defenseless?"

"And I appreciate you saving me. Twice. But I can't tell you anything else, so isn't it more important to catch that creep and find clues at the accident?"

"The scene and *Suit Man* aren't my priority. *You* are."

His blue eyes searched hers. If she'd known what he needed to hear, she would have said it. But she was a little frightened or worried or maybe just confused from the blow to her ear.

What was she thinking? These men had rammed her car off the road with the intention to kill her. And in all probability they had killed the man she'd been trying to help.

"I'll concede that you don't know me, but I'm not defenseless." The soreness in her jaw screamed otherwise. "I can take care of myself."

"Not tonight." He stepped back, one hand pushing through a thick head of short, light brown hair. "I'm escorting you home until someone decides what to do with you."

THE SHERIFF

ANGI MORGAN

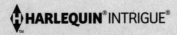
HARLEQUIN® INTRIGUE®

Thanks so much, Jan, you've been a
rock star this year. Jill and Allison,
your understanding and support is
unsurpassed.

ISBN-13: 978-0-373-74862-4

The Sheriff

Copyright © 2015 by Angela Platt

Recycling programs
for this product may
not exist in your area.

Printed in U.S.A.

™ www.Harlequin.com

Angi Morgan writes Harlequin Intrigue novels "where honor and danger collide with love." She combines actual Texas settings with characters who are in realistic and dangerous situations. Angi and her husband live in north Texas, with only the four-legged "kids" left in the house to interrupt her writing. They recently began volunteering for a local Labrador retriever foster program. Visit her website, angimorgan.com, or hang out with her on Facebook.

Books by Angi Morgan

Harlequin Intrigue

Hill Country Holdup
.38 Caliber Cover-up
Dangerous Memories
Protecting Their Child
The Marine's Last Defense

Texas Family Reckoning
Navy SEAL Surrender
The Renegade Rancher

West Texas Watchmen
The Sheriff

CAST OF CHARACTERS

Pete Morrison—Acting Sheriff of Presidio County, Texas. Adopted by a deputy who became sheriff, he was raised at the department and has been in law enforcement since high school.

Andrea Allen—Working on her PhD in Star Studies. A daughter who would like to succeed without the help of either of her very successful parents. If she finishes her paper, she can secure a job at one of the top observatories in the world.

Joe Morrison—Retired as sheriff after suffering a heart attack. He adopted Pete twenty-five years ago. Everyone in Marfa knows and loves him. But everyone has secrets.

Honey & Peach—Sisters who dispatch for the Presidio County Sheriff's Department.

Commander Tony Allen—Andrea's father, a former astronaut working for Homeland Security's Customs and Border Protection Office.

Cord McCrea—Texas Ranger and ranch owner, head of the newly formed West Texas task force tracking drug and gun runners.

Sharon—An undergrad working at the McDonald Observatory.

Patrice—A woman who delivers messages for the drug/gun runners.

Mr. Rook—A sadistic man of perfection who plays chess like he's playing with people's lives.

Chapter One

"This is not happening. Aliens are landing and I can't find the camera."

Lights moved in an erratic pattern low in the sky. Not aliens, but it was fun to think so. Someone on the ground? No. The lights were moving too swiftly. It had to be a chopper. It could not be a phenomenon. And especially not a UFO.

Andrea Allen was very familiar with everything that flew. She had to be when she was the only child of an astronaut and a pretty good pilot herself. It was definitely not a plane. It didn't look like a chopper, but it had to be. The lights weren't in the correct place. It hovered and disappeared.

Pulling the cords from her ears, she heard the faint drumbeat of "Bohemian Rhapsody" rocking in the background, but no mechanical sounds echoing in the distance. She rubbed her eyes and found the hovering object with the telescope. Whatever it was, it just wasn't producing enough light to distinguish an outline above the desert with a mountain ridge in the background.

Normally, she was bored out of her mind with the study on the Marfa Lights. Even though several tourists had posted seeing activity recently, no one with credentials had verified anything. Tourists posted all the time. Didn't they know it was just an occurrence similar to the aurora borealis? Everyone had heard of the northern lights, right?

The UT students studying the local phenomenon from the McDonald Observatory got excited, clamoring for a turn to watch the uneventful sky. Three nights later with no activity, everyone assumed the sighting had been taillights from the highway and then they all wanted the weekend off for a party.

Bored. Tonight had been no exception.

Nothing happened in this West Texas desert except lots of star time. Which she loved. She loved it a lot. Much more than she missed friends and family. Staring at a clear night sky was something even her astronaut dad didn't understand.

Since it hadn't been her night to stare through a telescope at the far distant universe, her coworker Sharon had begged Andrea to take her place on the university study. Sharon wanted the night off because she had a hot date with her boyfriend, Logan. Granted, the young student had been here three nights in a row, since it was part of her class assignment. Andrea didn't mind. She needed to switch sleeping to days anyway.

Another sparkle of red twinkled. Just a bit closer than the last spot.

With her spare hand she dug around in the disorganized bag her coworker had dropped in her front seat before leaving the observatory. "Where's that silly camera?"

She lost sight of the floating light through the scope and bounced her gaze to the horizon. Nothing. Had it disappeared?

If the darn thing came back, she needed the camera to record it. Dumping the satchel upside down, she searched through the assortment of items that resembled a loose picnic basket. Snacks, bottles of water, gum wrappers, a notepad, a small tripod, a spoon to go along with the empty yogurt containers, three different bags of candy—the butterscotch made her pause and unwrap a piece to stick in her mouth. No video camera.

She scooped everything back into Sharon's UFO-watching sack.

Where's the camera? It was just here. She closed her eyes to visualize getting in the car. Sharon had run outside with the bag in her hand as the car backed out of the parking space. The window had been down. "Passenger side. It must have fallen under the seat."

"My gosh." The adrenaline rush grew each time she saw the light a bit closer. A burst of red. A burst of blue. A plane would have red or green running lights on its wings and a white strobe light would be a consistent flash. A chopper, same thing. There were ways to identify what was in the air. Flight patterns.

Amazed, she just stared.

"Camera!" She ran to the car, pausing when she caught sight of the red flash again. She still couldn't distinguish an outline of what was flying haphazardly and low to the ground. It couldn't be a UFO. There were no such things.

Did she really believe that? No life in the universe other than on Earth? No time to debate, she needed pictures. Lots of pictures and evidence.

No one was around for miles to break into Sharon's tiny compact car, so it wasn't locked. The keys were still even in the ignition. Andrea yanked open the door, immediately feeling under the seat. "Gotcha!"

The strap was caught on something. The sky behind her was empty as she switched to the backseat, dropping to her knees again to get low enough to search.

If she could obtain evidence of the Marfa Lights, she could publish in addition to her PhD, make a name for herself as an astronomer. Finally be worthy of her Allen heritage. It all hinged on concrete evidence. Could it happen? She recognized the sudden nausea and shakiness as fear. Fear of jumping to conclusions and being discredited. She'd verify the facts.

"What am I thinking? I have my own study to

finish. I'm not chasing another subject. This is university work. I. Can't. Switch. Again." Her teeth ground against each other in frustration—not only with the silly camera strap, but also with the lack of focus her parents had accused her of. "What is this stuck on?"

The flashlight was back on the viewing platform with the UFO bag, and the dome light had been out for months. She couldn't really see anything under the seat, even bent at another awkward angle. But she finally came up with the handheld video camera, pressing Record and immediately scanning the sky for her mystery lights.

Andrea maneuvered from the tiny car, resting the camera on the door frame. "I don't know if it's appropriate to talk while recording, but I think it's better to describe what I'm seeing. Mainly because I don't know what I'm seeing. Five minutes ago there were flashing lights. Nothing about it suggests standard aircraft. And yet nothing suggests the Marfa phenomenon."

The corner of her eye caught a blur, something running from the darkness in her direction. She swung the camera toward it.

"I can't tell what that is. For the record, I'm Andrea Allen and alone out here. There's nothing close at hand to defend myself from wild animals or— Good grief, what is that?"

She kept recording, squinted. Still couldn't make it out. "The lights have disappeared. I don't know what's weaving toward me, but I think I'm going to get back in the car and roll up the windows."

Proud of herself for continuing the recording, she felt with one hand until finding the window handle. It was the first time she was grateful she'd paid extra for electric windows. But she wasn't in her car, she was in Sharon's old sedan. Backseat ready, she pushed the lock and shut it, then moved to the front door.

During the transfer, she lost where the movement was, spotting it again when she found the handle. Closer. More in focus. A man. Staggering.

She dropped the camera on the seat, using both hands to tug at the window stuck on the old car. "Not now. Uh. Give me a break."

"Help."

"Help? Not likely." She ran to the driver's side. If she couldn't get locked inside her car, she didn't have to stay there.

Marfa was nine miles away. This was a police matter.

"Please. Help. Night of aliens."

She heard him loud and clear as he tripped and stumbled into her. Shirtless, his skin horribly dirty. His lips parched and cracked. With his short-cropped military cut, she could see the gaping wound on the side of his head. There were cuts and bruises all over his arms. Some fresh, some old.

Where was the nearest hospital? Alpine. She couldn't leave him.

He fell into her arms, knocking her into the car frame. She kept him moving, guiding his fall onto the backseat. She pushed at his legs, tried folding them so the door would close.

"Come on, man. Help me...out...here." He was unresponsive and most likely unconscious. She ran to the other door, forgetting it was locked, wasting precious time reaching through the window. She yanked and pulled until he budged enough to bend his knees on top of his body and shut both doors. It had to be uncomfortable, but the man wasn't complaining.

"Hospital!"

She left everything on the viewing platform, including her cell phone, only having a moment of disappointment about not documenting evidence. This guy was clearly not from a UFO. It looked as if he'd been in the desert for days.

There was no question the man's life was much more important than any research. She pointed the car east toward Alpine. Marfa was closer and had a doctor but no hospital. The dashboard lights showed smudges of the man's blood on her hands and forearms. She felt the stickiness of a heavy damp saturation just above her hip.

"Are you bleeding to death?" she screamed at the unconscious stranger and threw on the brakes. "Were you attacked by coyotes or something?"

Twisting to look at him closer, she searched the middle compartment for anything, even napkins.

There was nothing here to stem the loss of blood. She pulled her long-sleeve shirt over her head and shifted to reach his body, searching with her hands until she found a wound. Her fingers found a distinct puncture. She'd never seen one in real life, but there was no mistaking the bullet hole.

Dear Lord. "What happened to you?"

She pressed the shirt into his side, moving his arm into a position to hold it in place. He moaned.

"Thank God you're alive, but who knows how long that will last."

The lights were closer, then gone again.

Using all the training her father had taught her about control, she forced her thoughts to slow and hold herself together. She readjusted in the seat and buckled the seat belt in place before putting the car in Drive.

One at a time, she swiped her hands across her jeans to remove the man's damp blood before pulling out of the parking lot. She dipped her head to her shoulder, trying to push a loose piece of hair, stuck across her cheek, off her sweaty face.

What in the world was she getting involved in? A secret chopper? Maybe a new stealth plane? "Are you military or something? I sure hope you're not a fugitive or a drug runner. But whoever you are, you're dying and I have to get you to a hospital."

Nothing was around for miles. No homes, no businesses, no help. *Help?* She should call for help. Where was her stupid phone?

Oh, no. It was in the chair where she'd dumped Sharon's bag. She needed to call, tell someone she had an injured man and get directions to the hospital in Alpine. She turned in the small lot, prepared to jump from the car and dial on the way back. A one- or two-minute delay was better than getting lost. Maybe they could send an ambulance to meet her.

Bright spotlights blinded her in all her mirrors. She couldn't see and tilted the rearview up. *Forget the phone.* She punched the gas and could smell the smoking rubber of the slightly balding tires.

"It's following us!" Whatever *it* was, it was practically on top of the trunk.

The road was straight so she couldn't stop or it would crash into her. There was no way to outrun it in an old four-cylinder economy.

"Now what?"

Colored lights flashed. The inside of the car looked like a blinking neon sign. She could barely see the two-lane highway, and then whatever followed rammed the little car. Andrea's neck jerked back. Her body smashed against the seat belt. Her wrists slammed into the steering wheel. Her father would be proud she didn't scream—as much as she wanted to let out a string of obscenities at whoever was flying that thing.

Another hit. The thing had to be a chopper. The man in her backseat had to be in serious trouble and now so was she.

The car skidded sideways onto the shoulder and

beyond. She maintained her grip, steering through the grass on the side of the highway. The chopper blocked her path back to the road. They bounced a few seconds before she aimed at the wire between fence posts and gunned the little engine again.

She had no idea what was out here. She could be headed straight to a small boulder or a ravine. The unknown was definitely frightening, but not as much as the chopper on her tail.

As suddenly as the thing appeared behind her, it was gone. No lights. No sounds. She wanted to slow down, but it wasn't safe. Too late she wished she had when a slab of broken foundation forced the car sideways.

It rolled.

She screamed.

Chapter Two

Driving this empty length of pavement could put him to sleep if he wasn't careful. Pete Morrison stretched his neck from side to side, turned the squad car's radio up a bit louder and rolled down the window for fresh air. A quick trip out to the Lights Viewing Area and back to the office for some shut-eye.

Probably just a plane and a waste of taxpayer gas.

"I saw some strange stuff out there," a trucker had told Dispatch. "I don't believe in UFOs or nothing like that, but if it is, I want the credit for seeing it first. Okay?"

"Sure thing" had been the standard reply to every driver who thought he'd seen a UFO. And each report had to be checked out. It was Marfa, after all.

Griggs would get an earful in the morning about honesty and the law. This was the third time in two weeks Pete had covered the son of a gun's night shift at the last minute because of *illness*. Everyone knew the deputy had gone to Alpine to party. If he wanted to change shifts, he just needed to ask. There were twelve other deputies on the payroll, and yet Pete was covering. Again.

Partying hadn't been something he'd personally wanted to do for the past couple of months. But since Griggs had transferred from Jefferson Davis County, he'd been covering his shifts a lot. Covering wasn't the problem. He got extra pay and could normally sleep on the back cot. Nothing ever happened in Marfa beyond speeding citations and public intoxication.

Tonight was one of the exceptions. He'd make a quick pass by the official Marfa Lights Viewing Area, drive back and get some shut-eye.

"Dispatch, I've got an all clear. Not seeing anything unusual. But I might as well make a run to the county line."

"Okey dokey, Pete. This is Peach. See you in a while."

He laughed at Peach's official acknowledgment. No sense trying to get her to change. Everyone called her Peach. She insisted on it. Her sister, Honey, got the day shift since she was older. He supposed nicknames were better than Winafretta and Wilhilmina. They'd been in Dispatch for as long as his dad had been a deputy or sheriff of Presidio County. Or longer. His dad swore no one could remember hiring either of them. They'd just shown up one day.

When his dad officially retired, the new sheriff

could request replacements for them, but he'd like to see anyone tell Peach she was too old to handle things at night around the office. A shot of regret lodged like a clump of desert dirt in his throat. He'd have to withdraw his name from the election so someone else would step forward. Galen Rooney had only been on the force for a couple of years and just didn't have the experience needed to run things.

No matter who the county elected, they'd most likely keep him on as a deputy. If not… Unfortunately, he hadn't thought past quitting the race. The idea of withdrawing gnawed at his gut like a bad case of food poisoning. He'd never quit anything. His dad—he couldn't ever think of the man who'd raised him as anything else—wouldn't be happy.

"Crap. What the hell was that?"

He successfully dodged a long object in the middle of the road. He swiftly U-turned the squad car, flipped his lights on and drove a couple of seconds. Parking across the road, he turned the floodlight until it shone on a black bumper resting on the yellow line.

Joe Morrison had raised him riding shotgun in a squad car. The mental checklist of what he did exiting his vehicle was as natural as walking. Even if Peach wasn't a stickler for the rules, he still needed to let her know exactly what he was doing.

"Dispatch, I swung back west to pick up some road debris. Guess a bumper dropped from a car and the driver didn't stop to take care of it. Almost sent me off the road."

"Wow, Sheriff Pete. It's a good thing we got that call to take you out that way tonight, then," Peach replied through the speaker. "What if an eighteen-wheeler had hit that thing? Oh, gosh, and what if it had been transporting fuel or hazardous waste? It might have spilled and leached into the water supply. We could have had deformed livestock or mutant wolves running around for years without anyone knowing."

"You reading another end-of-the-world novel, Peach?"

"How did you know?" she asked.

"Lucky guess." He laughed into the microphone. Peach and Honey's theories of espionage and Armageddon changed daily with each book they read.

"Well, I'm at a good spot in the story, so I'll let you clear the garbage. Shout out when you're heading back," she said.

"You got it. And, Peach, will you stop with the sheriff title? You know I'm the acting sheriff until the election."

"I feel the same way about my dispatch title."

"Point taken."

Picking up the plastic bumper from a small car, he noticed some skid marks on the asphalt. He flipped his flashlight on and followed their path to the gravel and farther into the flattened knee-high grass. A vehicle had obviously gone off the road. He tossed the bumper to the side and started walking.

About twenty yards away, the fence wasn't only down, but a section had been demolished and disappeared. There was nothing in range of the flashlight beam, so he shut off the light and let his eyes adjust to the well-lit night.

He finally spotted the car, the underbelly reflecting the starlight about four hundred yards into the field. He ran the short distance to the vehicle. The driver might need a hospital. A serious injury, he'd need to transport himself.

"Dispatch." Back in his car, he pointed the spotlight directly in front of the hood and followed the path through the fence. "Peach?" He raised his voice to get her attention.

"I'm here, just finishing the chapter. You heading back?"

"Looks like a vehicle went off the road about half a mile east of the Viewing Area. I spotted it. Driving there now. Check if there are any cattle around that could get loose, and notify the owner."

"Time to wake the sheriff."

"Don't wake Dad. He's officially retired."

"You know that's not going to stop him. Neither could a heart attack."

"Give me five minutes to check out the vehicle, Peach." And do something on his own without his dad shouting instructions in his ear. "I need to find the driver and see if we need assistance."

"He's gonna be mad," she sang into the radio. "You know how he hates to be the last told."

"My call."

"But you know how he is," she whined.

"Remember that he's retired. Five minutes."

"Yes, sirree-dee, Acting Sheriff Morrison."

Yeah, but for how long? He watched the land closest to him, searching for ditches or large rocks. Closer to the vehicle, it was apparent it had hit the foundation of an old building. Whoever had been driving the car had been traveling at a high speed, hit the broken concrete and flipped the vehicle.

He approached with caution, flashlight in hand, gun at his fingertips. "County Sheriff. Anyone need help?"

No answer. Nothing but the cool wind.

He switched the flashlight, looked inside the car. One body. Nonresponsive.

"Sir?" He felt the man's neck for a pulse. "Damn." Dead.

The body was mangled pretty badly. "You should have buckled up, stranger. How'd you end up in the backseat?" He'd seen weirder things happen in car accidents than the driver being thrown around.

Back at his car, he pulled his radio through the open window. "Peach, send for an ambulance. We have a fatality."

"Poor soul."

"Yeah." He tossed the microphone onto the seat.

"Unit says they're about an hour out, Pete," he

heard through the speaker. "There was an accident in Alpine and since it's only a pickup they aren't in a hurry."

"Not a problem."

No shut-eye anytime soon. He was stuck waiting here an hour unless Peach called him for a Marfa emergency. Fat chance. He'd get the pics they'd need for their records and maybe catch a nap after. He grabbed the camera from the Tahoe.

Careful not to disturb the body, he started snapping away, including the outside of the car and the tags. When he reached the driver's-side door, he noticed blood on the outside and then the tracks, patterns in the dirt as if someone had crawled from the car.

"Anyone out here?" he yelled, tilting the beam as far as it would project and following distinct shoe impressions. "I'm with the Marfa Sheriff's Department and here to help."

He shoved the camera in his pocket and picked up his pace. Two or three minutes passed, the footprints grew more erratic and then the bottom of a shoe came into view.

"Hello?" He ran to a woman lying facedown in the sand. She was visibly breathing, but unresponsive to shaking her shoulder. He verified no broken bones and no wounds, then rolled her over.

There was a lot of blood on her white tank, but no signs of any bleeding. He dusted the sand from her young face. Smooth skin. *That won't go in the report*. Caucasian. Short brown hair. Blue eyes, responsive to light.

"Ma'am? Can you hear me?"

The accident couldn't have happened that long ago. The hood of the car had been warm. Should he move her? There could be multiple things wrong with her. He ran his hands over her body checking for broken bones. She wasn't responding to stimulation. She needed immediate care and the ambulance was an hour out. That sealed it. He scooped her into his arms and rushed her back to his car.

Once he had her buckled, he picked up the microphone. "Peach!"

He returned along the same tire tracks, picking up his speed since he knew the path was clear.

"Bored already?" Peach asked.

"I'm transporting a survivor to Alpine General. Found her fifty yards or so from the car."

"Lord have mercy. I'll let them know you're on your way."

The car hit a bump and he heard a moan and mumbling from next to him. Good sign. "Hang in there, ma'am."

Slowing as he hit the road's pavement, he could swear the woman begged him not to let the aliens get her.

The Marfa Lights sure did attract a lot of kooks.

Chapter Three

"I've told you several times now, I'm not sure what rammed me off the road. It had to be a chopper, but the lights blinded me and I never got a good look at what model."

Everyone seemed to know the man who had brought Andrea to the hospital. He leaned his broad shoulders against the wall closest to the door. He'd scribbled notes and asked questions while the doctors looked her over. And almost every other sentence had been spent correcting someone congratulating him for his new position as sheriff.

Pardon, *acting* sheriff.

A sprained wrist, a minor concussion and dirty clothes, that was the extent of her accident injuries. Her favorite jeans were ruined. Not to mention Sharon's car.

The nurse said she could get her a hospital gown, but the good-looking deputy hadn't offered to leave the room while she changed. Ruined and filthy clothes would just have to do. She'd feel too open and exposed in front of *Acting* Sheriff Pete Morrison.

It was hardly fair to have such an attractive lawman interrogating her. It made her mind wander to forbidden topics, so it was much safer to remain completely covered.

"How tall are you?" he asked, flipping another page in his notebook.

"Five-nine. How could that be important?" As tall as she was, she'd have to tiptoe to kiss him. What was wrong with her thinking? Had she hit her head a little too hard? Of course she had. Hello. Concussion!

"Just being thorough."

She watched him sort of hide a grin, draw his brows together in concentration and drop his gaze to her chest. So he'd noticed the pink bra? No worries. Why? *Because he's extremely cute, that's why.*

"You're certain you didn't hear anything? The man who 'came from the desert,' as you put it, he didn't say anything?" he asked.

"I don't think so. By the way, how is that guy doing? Is he still in surgery? I keep asking, but no one seems to know anything about him. This is the only hospital, right?"

The nurse looked confused when Andrea had asked earlier. This time she turned to the sheriff, who shook his head, then shrugged. Everyone coming into the room had looked to the young sheriff for permission to speak and been denied.

"Can you tell us who your friend is?" he asked, flashing bright blue eyes her direction.

"Check your notes, Sheriff Morrison. I'm certain I told you he wasn't my friend. That was sometime between having my temperature taken and my wrist x-rayed."

"Yes, ma'am, you did say that." The sheriff looked at his notes and flipped to the previous page. "No need to call me Sheriff. Pete will do."

"Guess there's nothing wrong with her memory, Pete," the nurse said as she continued to wrap Andrea's left hand, pausing several times to smile at the hunky man.

Andrea had regained consciousness in the emergency room with a horrible smell wafting under her nose. It wasn't her first time for smelling salts. She'd gotten rammed a couple of times as a shortstop on the softball field in college. She could just imagine what her mother would say when she told her parents about this sprain. Peggy Allen would be glad her daughter was uninjured and it was simply a miracle how her middle daughter had managed to avoid a car accident until the ripe old age of twenty-six.

Not a miracle to her father, who had taught her how to drive like a naval aviator late for a launch at NASA. That was a phone call she dreaded. At least it could wait until morning. No sense worrying her parents tonight.

"How's that, Miss Allen?" the nurse asked, securing the last bit of elastic bandage around her wrist.

Miraculously—to use her mother's word—the slight ache was the only pain she experienced. Other than a headache from the concussion.

"Great. Thanks. Can I go now?"

"I just need to get the doctor's signature and I can get your discharge papers." The nurse put her supplies away, smiled prettily again at the annoying officer. "See you, Pete."

"What's your hurry?" the good-looking man asked as she left.

At first she thought he was flirting with the nurse. He dipped his dimpled chin, raised his eyebrows, expectantly waiting...

"Oh, you mean me? I'm not overly fond of hospitals." Oh, Lordy, he really had a dimpled chin. She was a sucker for that little cleft under rugged, nice lips. *Whoa.*

How could his straight brows rise even higher? It was as if getting asked a question made him feel guilty for not answering, or he assumed she'd seen a lot of hospitals. Either way, she immediately regretted giving the officer any insight into her character. "The answer to your question, Sheriff, is no. I haven't escaped from a loony bin. I told you, I'm a PhD candidate working at the McDonald Observatory."

"I didn't say a word."

"Your face says enough without your lips moving." She covered her mouth with her good hand to make herself shut up. The annoying man just laughed and grinned even bigger. "What are you waiting on, anyway? I told you I can phone and get a ride home. The student I was covering for is already in Alpine. Somewhere."

He pulled a cell from his pocket. "Use mine."

She held her hand out, wincing at the soreness already setting into her muscles. It didn't matter, she had no idea what Sharon's number was without recovering her cell from the Viewing Area.

"I don't know her number."

She hated to think what a cab ride to the north side of Fort Davis would cost. If they even had cabs in Alpine, Texas, that traveled the fifty miles or so outside the city. She'd probably have to bribe the driver by paying him double.

"We tried to locate the owner of the car, but the listing is in Austin."

"I did mention she's a student."

He stood straighter, slipping the cell back in his chest pocket. "To answer your question, I'm still here because I need your official statement and I thought you might need a ride back to wherever you're staying in Fort Davis."

"Oh. Thanks. That's very considerate of you. I'm at the observatory, actually. I guess you do things differently here."

"Spent a lot of time with the law back home?"

She just stared at him. The man was actually being extremely nice. And seemed to be charming. Part of his expressive nature, she surmised.

"We'd never get along." She clamped her hand over her mouth again.

"I don't know about that. I like a woman who speaks her mind. Kinda refreshing."

"They gave me a pain pill. It must have gone straight to my mouth."

He nodded and covered a grin by rubbing long fingers over his lips. "I was here before the pain pill. You weren't exactly holding back then, either."

For some reason she wanted to push her hands through his slightly mussed hair and see the sandy waviness up close. *Wow.* What had the doctors given her to make her think like this? She had to remain professional.

"Do you think I did something wrong, Sheriff?"

"Miss Allen—"

"Please, my name's Andrea." She checked out her torn black jeans and ragged undershirt still stained with blood, not feeling like a Miss anything.

"Andrea. We've done some checking."

"Don't tell me, there weren't any planes or helicopters flying in that area. So I actually saw a UFO." She was trying to be cutesy or sarcastic or just funny. A giggle even escaped, but the expression on the officer's face didn't indicate that he was laughing with her. In fact, he looked dead serious. "I'm joking, you know."

"You did mention that aliens were chasing you."

"I was referring to illegal immigrants. Or maybe I was just delirious from being knocked out cold. I never once seriously thought I was being chased by an extraterrestrial, something foreign to this modern age of flying machines. I study the stars. I don't live in them." Exhausted, she wanted to lie back on the examining table and sleep. "I'm here working on my last dissertation."

The room tilted. Or maybe she did. It was hard to tell. She was conscious of falling, knew it was about to happen before it did. The heaviness of her arms prevented her from stopping herself. She didn't hit the floor.

Instead, a firm grip kept her in place, then lowered her to the pillow.

He had the best hands. Strong, short practical nails. Firm. And she shouldn't forget how quick. He'd taken a step and caught her as she swayed.

"Maybe we should talk later?"

"I'm sorry, Sheriff." She rubbed her head and winced at the little bump. "I'm...sort...of...woozy."

"Not a problem. I'm not going anywhere. And it's Pete."

"I'm Andrea." She could really get into liking that mouth of his. "You have a super-cute smile. Did I—" A yawn escaped and she almost couldn't remember what she was saying. "Oh, yeah. Did I tell you I like your smile?"

"I think you did, Miss Allen. I think you need to get some shut-eye."

She turned into his hand, still holding her shoulder. She caught a clean, musky scent before letting her heavy eyelids close and stay that way. "Can't think of a better place to do it."

THE SHERIFF WHO'D taken Andrea's statement stood outside the door, which was open just a crack. The person he spoke to was in scrubs. Maybe the nurse who'd checked her out earlier, maybe someone new. Shoot, it could be the doctor there to discharge her. She didn't know. She grabbed the side of the bed and began pushing herself upright, jerking to a stop as a hiss of pain whistled between her teeth.

"Wow, that really hurts." Her wrist was bandaged. Funny, she could remember everything except that her wrist was sprained.

"I'm headed back to the scene," Pete said. "I'm waiting on the local PD who are going to stay with Miss Allen until we have a few more facts."

"What if we need the room?"

"Mrs. Yardly, it might be a Friday night in downtown Alpine, but when was the last time the ER filled up?"

The casual stance and charm disappeared quickly as a balding man approached, flipping open a flat wallet. The kind she'd seen many times before.

The Suit Man seemed to have no personality. He wasn't attempting to make friends. His straight, thin lips never curved into an approachable welcome. "Steven Manny, Department of Homeland Security. I'm here for Andrea Allen."

"I was told local police would be here to escort

her to the observatory," the sheriff answered, shifting his right hand near the top of his gun.

"I have a few questions and will make certain she gets returned to her residence. You're relieved." A light knuckle tap on the door and Suit Man walked inside. "Miss Allen, are you ready?"

She nodded but locked eyes with Pete, silently imploring the sheriff not to leave her alone. Before she verbalized the words, he stepped into the room behind the new guy and closed the door.

"She passed out a few minutes ago and they're not ready to discharge her."

"We understand your concern, but we're moving. Now. Miss Allen." He gestured for her to head to the door.

As anxious as she was to escape the hospital before landing in Pete's arms, she was scared to leave without him. The guy demanding she put on her shoes wasn't the average government-issued suit.

"Where are we going?" she asked.

"That's classified."

"I won't tell anyone." Pete seemed taller, firmer. He waved his hand for her to stay put. "Think you can give me another look at your badge?"

When Pete took another step, ready to do battle, the Suit shoved his forearm across the sheriff's windpipe. Andrea jumped to her feet to help but received a backhand with the Suit's free arm, knocking her across the small emergency room bed.

Pete was no slouch. He was younger, three or four

inches taller and in really good shape. His strength kicked in and he shoved Suit Man straight into the path of her hospital-socked feet. Without shoes she couldn't do much damage, but she did put a heel in Suit Man's gut, hurtling him into the supply cabinet.

Pete was there, swung his left fist and connected with Suit Man's jaw, sending him flying backward into the door. Her rescuer swung again, connected a second time. She recognized the panic in Suit Man's eyes. He knew he'd failed.

Suit Man had something in one hand and the other hand on the door handle.

"Watch out!" she yelled.

Pete ducked, but she couldn't get out of the path. The metal hit her square in the ear, and she tumbled to the linoleum.

There was some yelling, really close to her ear, but the world was spinning sufficiently enough that it didn't register. She saw the blur of black dress shoes running from the room. It was all she could do to focus on not passing out. Then the strong arms she admired lifted her to the table.

"Everything okay in here, Pete?" the voice she'd heard earlier from the hall asked through the intercom.

"Yardly, I need a doctor, and where's security?"

"It's just a bump. My ears are ringing. That's all." She'd seen double for a few seconds, but that had already passed. "What are you waiting for?"

A nurse and then a doctor entered. Pete slipped

out, but she could hear his raised voice in the hall. She saw his phone to his ear. Watched him pace in front of the rectangle of a window and then speak with the doctor before coming back in the room.

"Why aren't you chasing Suit Man?" she asked between the blood pressure cuff and insisting she was fine.

"You're stuck with me while I ensure your safety. That's your best option." He didn't seem at all satisfied being saddled with the position of her protector.

"I can wait for the police. There are plenty of people here. So go."

"You're serious?" He followed the nurse to the door, looked down the hall and slammed it shut. "Someone's trying to kill you and you want me to leave you here, defenseless?"

"And I appreciate your saving me. Twice. But I can't tell you anything else, so isn't it more important to catch that creep and find clues at the accident?"

"The scene and *Suit Man* aren't my priority. *You* are."

She watched his Adam's apple bob nicely as he swallowed hard. His blue eyes searched hers. If she'd known what he needed to hear, she would have said it. But she was a little frightened or worried or maybe just confused from the blow to her ear.

What was she thinking? These men had rammed her car off the road trying to kill her. Okay, technically, it was Sharon's car. And in all probability, they had killed the man she'd been trying to help. She'd been knocked silly-unconscious by a complete stranger with really good counterfeit DHS credentials who also wasn't afraid to show his face and try to kill her with security cameras everywhere.

"I'll concede that you don't know me, but I'm not *defenseless*." The soreness in her jaw screamed otherwise. "He caught me off guard. That's all. I can take care of myself."

"Not tonight." He stepped back, one hand going to his hip and the other pushing through a thick head of short, light brown hair. "I'm escorting you home until someone decides what to do with you. The local authorities will find Suit Man."

"Are you sure about that?"

She'd lost her chance. He'd made his decision. And it was probably best. The only personal possessions she still had were her earphones. They'd hooked around her neck and somehow not fallen off. If she'd been alone when the *Suit* attacked, she would have been dead before she could press the nurse call button.

Or maybe worse. She might have actually been woozy enough to leave with him. Then what?

The sheriff opened the door. "Yardly!" The nurse he'd been speaking to came running. "We're not waiting to give an incident report. We're leaving. Do what you have to do to get us out of here. *Now*."

"Well then…it isn't just another boring Friday night, after all."

Chapter Four

Pete kept Andrea Allen in sight through the sliver of an opening in the door. There weren't any windows in the exam room, and he needed to keep an eye on her. Victim or perpetrator. He didn't know if that was an unsuccessful rescue attempt or an averted abduction.

Whichever, something didn't sit right and he wanted to know what she was doing. She was the prime suspect or witness in a man's death.

"I've got things under control, Dad. I don't need backup at the hospital. I'll be gone before anyone can get here. We're just waiting on a prescription. There's nothing you can do. I know you're already at the office. Just stay there and handle that end of things. When exactly did Peach call you?"

"Now, son, it's no reflection on your abilities that she called. We've been working together for a couple of decades."

When were any of his instructions going to be followed?

He'd been at the hospital almost three hours waiting on Andrea to be treated and discharged before Suit Man—it was as good a description as any—had shown up. And to get the okay for her to leave was taking a lot longer than he'd anticipated. The murderers seemed to be a lot more organized than the hospital staff, who couldn't get them out the door.

"Who am I kidding? Peach called the *real sheriff* as soon as I reported the dead body. Right?" A guy who went missing by the time the ambulance showed up twenty minutes later.

"You are the sheriff now and never mind how long I've been here," his father said, sounding wide-awake and probably on his third cup of coffee. He'd dodged answering like he usually did. "The picture you sent popped a red flag. I'm waiting on a call from the DEA and DHS."

"You think this guy was working undercover?" His charge was lying on an ER bed, ice bag on her ear.

"Could be, Pete. They're waking up some top-dog bureaucrat to get instructions. I don't want the call to drop on my way out to the Viewing Area. But I want to take a look at that car before it disappears, too."

"So you believe our Sleeping Beauty's story about the flashing lights?" His dad would take over the crime scene while Pete babysat the witness. This night just kept getting better and better.

"Well, something's not right. Dead bodies don't

just walk away. The paramedics are sure there was no sign of animal involvement?" his dad asked.

"They actually accused me of yanking their chain when they returned to the hospital." A quick look into the room confirmed Andrea was still asleep, secure and safe.

"Then whoever was in the chopper chasing our witness didn't want the body found."

"Did Peach get anyone at the observatory to verify her ID?"

"Yeah, the director confirmed everything. She's lucky you got there as soon as you did or she'd be dead twice over now. Don't let her out of your sight until we get this thing figured out."

"I hadn't planned to. I know my job, Dad." He wasn't normally a pacer, but he couldn't lean against the wall much longer. He looked at the nurses' station, where there was still no sign of activity.

"You'll make a fine replacement. I'm looking forward to sleeping in," his dad said.

"That'll never happen. You'll just be at the café for breakfast earlier." He left the replacement statement hanging. He couldn't get into a conversation they'd been avoiding for almost six weeks while in the middle of what was becoming a major mess. "Listen, you know you're supposed to take it easy. I'll stop by the crash site on my way back."

"I'm not an invalid."

"You should be after a quadruple bypass."

Andrea yanked the door open.

"He's dead?" She was obviously panicked, more upset than she'd been earlier after the Suit had back-handed her jaw. "The man who stumbled out of the desert is dead? Did he die in the crash? Did I kill him?"

"Gotta run, Dad. Get a deputy there to pick you up. You shouldn't be driving." He slid the cell into his pocket and faced her. "I'm sorry you had to hear like that. How he died wasn't clear when I viewed the body, so I don't have the answer to your question."

"I need another shirt. Now."

He witnessed her realization she still wore the man's blood. Her chest began rising and falling more rapidly, and she was about to completely lose it. Good or bad? He didn't know. They didn't get too many cases like this bizarre situation in Jeff Davis County.

One second he was sticking his head out the door calling for clean scrubs and the next he saw Andrea tug the back of her shirt over her head.

"What are you doing?"

She threw the shirt across the room. "I think that's self-explanatory. What? You've never seen a woman in a bra before?"

"Here." He shifted the pillow from the bed to block the view of her breasts.

"I'm not claiming harassment, if you're worried—"

"This is a small town and people will talk no matter what you claim."

"Someone's trying to kill me. I have no idea why. And you're worried about seeing me in my bra." She stared at him, hugging the pillow to her stomach.

She wanted a logical explanation. There wasn't one. "They're covering their bases."

"But I don't know anything," she whispered.

"They don't know that."

The door swung open, and Ginny held a pair of pink scrubs. She handed them to him without a word and turned to leave.

"Wait." He stopped the nurse after the disapproving look she shot his way. "I'll leave and you help Miss Allen get cleaned up and changed. Bag all her clothes, will ya?"

"Sure, Pete." Ginny smiled, raising an eyebrow to match the questions in her voice.

He stepped outside and pulled the door shut behind him, leaning against the wall and refusing to beat his head against the drywall. He was attracted to Andrea Allen in a major way and needed to set it aside until this mess was cleared up.

It didn't matter that her belly had been faintly stained with blood. He'd barely been able to think like a sheriff while admiring her other...assets. His red-hot American boy shouted at him to take notice.

The woman he'd been watching closely was completely in shape, sleek muscles in spite of being a scholar. That is, they still needed to verify her identity. They hadn't found any ID at the scene. Nothing on the viewing platform the way she claimed.

And if he hadn't seen the dead man himself, they'd be questioning her story about that, too.

Maybe that's what she'd intended? Get him distracted so she could slip out of the hospital. Andrea Allen might just be a legitimate name she acquired so she could pretend to be someone from the university.

She was either the most carefree, speak-her-mind woman he'd ever met or the best con artist he'd ever witnessed. Being a looker helped. Spirited. Easily embarrassed on one hand and then contradicting it by stripping her shirt off without blinking an eye. Dark brown hair, skin that hadn't seen sun in a while and at least five necklaces, varying in length, drawing his stare to a pair of perfectly shaped breasts.

Ginny closed the door behind her. "She sure is upset that mystery guy is dead. You better watch her, Pete. No tellin' what you've stumbled across now. Guess that's the breaks when you're the sheriff." She dragged a finger across his nameplate. "Give me a call the next time you're in Alpine."

That ship had sailed a long time ago. "Thanks. Got an estimate on that prescription?"

"I'll go check for you."

He knocked on the door. Andrea sat on the bed, tapping the nails of her right hand on those of her left.

"So they think I'm crazy or lying. What do you think?" She had a pretty pout.

He shrugged and leaned on the wall again. "Maybe the man isn't dead after all. Maybe he came to and wandered into the desert. Search party will find him or evidence. They're usually good at that."

He cleared his throat, shifted his stance and forced his thoughts back to this case. A real case. A case that would prove he could be sheriff on his own merit. Not just because his dad had to step down after his heart attack. A case that would cinch an election.

He could hear questions being asked in the hall and no answers given to Ginny. But as much as the nurse kept her mouth shut here, he knew from first-hand experience she'd be sharing that he hadn't left the room. It would be all over the county as soon as she got on her social media devices.

So be it. Her gossiping was one of the reasons they'd stopped dating. Among other things.

If the woman he'd found had been caught in the wrong place, she needed protection. She could be a witness to a mysterious crime. Or part of it. He didn't know, but he would be discovering the truth soon.

Whatever was going on, until he figured it out, Andrea Allen was stuck with him.

BEING LOOPY IN the same room with a handsome man in uniform was humiliating enough. Then Andrea had taken her shirt off. *Oh, my gosh.* And he *was* handsome. She melted a bit when he put his hat on while leaving the hospital. *A cowboy? Really?* She was a rock 'n' roll girl all the way. Classic rock and definitely not country. This guy wore boots. Real boots. Still, she wanted to find out what kissing him was like.

She absolutely adored cleft chins. Especially this one. Then there were his eyes—kind and serious, or embarrassed and sweet.

"In case you're curious, we're heading down Highway 90 to Marfa instead of directly back 118 to Fort Davis. Just in case Suit Man is waiting with friends. There are plenty of cops on 90 tonight."

"Thanks."

She refused to further embarrass herself by making small talk. Her mouth had a habit of saying exactly what she was thinking, and the more time she thought about a subject, the more she'd end up blurting out trivia about herself.

"You warm enough?" he asked.

An innocent question. Small talk. She nodded, refusing to verbalize anything. It would open a floodgate of words that would inspire an entire conversation. And what if she ended up really liking him? How could he think of her as anything but a lunatic after what had happened?

"Sorry, is that an affirmative?"

"Yes." *Keep your cool. Maybe pretend to fall asleep and he won't ask anything.* She closed her eyes and leaned her head against the cool glass of the window, trying to see the stars and constellations.

"It's okay to talk, you know. Why don't you tell me about why you're in West Texas."

Was he just making conversation? Being polite? Or pumping her for information? Did it really matter? "I don't think I should say anything. You're treating me like a suspect."

"Do you feel like a suspect? I thought I was treating you like someone who needed a lift home. I do that. It's part of my job."

"I don't know why I'm being so paranoid."

"Maybe it has something to do with a dying man falling into your arms in the middle of nowhere or being chased by unknown assailants?" He scratched between his eyebrows for a brief second. He'd done that several times as he'd dipped his chin. "Or maybe it was the guy posing as Homeland Security who attacked you."

"Yeah." She laughed for a second, surprising herself. "That might have something to do with it."

"Pretty good badge, too. Had me fooled, even down to his shoes. Most of 'em forget the shoes."

She covered her eyes, sliding her hand over her mouth. *Small talk, remember the small talk consequences.* She did not want to reveal who her father was or who he worked for. His job title was a red flag, warning off guys too frightened to stand near him. Or others would fall into hero worship when the former astronaut showed up. Either of her father's personas would make her feel like the background, and she'd lose interest in a potential relationship.

"You can rest if you want. Use the blanket I took from the trunk for a pillow. I promise it's clean."

Rolling the dark cotton into a cylinder, her brain jump-started as the road veered directly west again. They were getting close to the Viewing Area. She could see warning lights down the road, still miles away, but bright for a clear night on a flat piece of earth. Not anything like what she'd experienced earlier.

"I probably should just keep my mouth shut, but I don't want to forget this." She pointed at the hills to the south. "The lights I saw first appeared back that direction. There was something strange about them."

"People see lights out here all the time."

"Don't dismiss me like a tourist."

"Pardon me, ma'am. I forgot for a minute you were an astrologer."

"Astronomer, but you already knew that. Trying to insult me?" From him, it didn't come across as an insult. "Can we stop to get my things, Pete? I think I'm clearheaded enough to have a discussion with your colleagues about what happened. And I'll never get to sleep if I don't have my music."

He tugged at the front of his shirt, shifting behind the wheel. "I don't think that's a good idea."

So when Pete didn't want her to know something or he was holding back, he kept a straight face and couldn't smile. Interesting. He was definitely holding back. She'd seen a lot of guys in uniform in her lifetime and they all stood a little straighter, forcing the confidence to come through as the truth.

"I don't really want to see Sharon's car or have that memory with me forever. But isn't it better than wondering about it for the rest of my life? Which is worse?"

"I can't answer that, Miss Allen." He pulled to the shoulder of the road and put the car in Park. "What I can tell you is that nothing was there except the car."

"You aren't taking me back to the observatory. Are you?"

"No, ma'am."

"So you think I murdered that man and wrecked my friend's car and made up a story about weird chopper lights to cover everything up? He was shot. Did you find a gun? And really, I came into the desert without anything? No cell, no purse, no shovel, no identification whatsoever to get rid of a dead man?" She'd started talking and couldn't stop. "Granted, if I were getting rid of a dead man, I probably wouldn't carry my ID. But alone? Get real. And if you knew me at all, no snacks and no water? Well, that just isn't going to happen."

"Wow." He draped his arm over the steering wheel, turning more of his body toward her and smiling once again. "That's impressive."

"I have a vivid imagination and think really fast. My dad rubbed off on me. I don't understand how you can assume that I'm guilty without any proof. There isn't any proof. Right? I mean, I'm not being framed, am I? Lots of people knew where I'd be tonight."

"Just hold on a minute." He straightened the arm closer to her, reaching out to pat her shoulder. "If you can take a breath and slow down to my speed, I can explain what's going on. To a certain degree."

She faced forward and shoved her fingers under her legs. Watching his sincerity was clouding her ability to analyze the situation correctly. She'd allowed him to distract her far too long and should have called her parents immediately. She knew *that* number by heart. "Okay, I'm breathing."

"You've been in protective custody since I got a phone call from the paramedics that there wasn't a body in the vehicle. No one's arresting you."

"But you saw him? I'm not…" She'd been about to say *crazy*.

He nodded. "I have pictures of a man at the scene matching the description you gave me earlier. Neither of us imagined it."

"Thank goodness." The sigh of relief was more than just verbal, it was liberating, and she physically felt lighter. For a moment, she'd doubted if she was experiencing an actual memory. Part of her imagination could have been distorted from the concussion.

Was that a possibility? She had definitely passed out after the accident. Could she have warped what really happened? Should she throw that scenario into the mix? No. She wasn't paranoid, just overthinking as usual. It was better to wait on the investigation and not doubt herself.

"Look, Miss Allen. Until we know what's going on, everyone believes it's better for me to stick close."

"I can't do my work just anywhere. Even under protective custody at the observatory would be difficult. Don't I have to consent or something? And who's everyone?"

For once, the man with all the answers seemed at a loss for words. It couldn't be plainer he was choosing his words carefully.

"I'm not trying to scare you, but being new around here you may not know that we've had a lot of drugs and guns crossing the border recently. Strange activity involving a helicopter and a disappearing body seems more than a little suspicious. It's better to be safe."

"And better to keep me close while you verify that I don't have anything to do with it."

"Hmm, there is that."

He grinned again, and she realized that there wasn't anything calculating about it. He seemed to be a good-looking, concerned officer who took his job very seriously to help her feel safe and at ease. Correction, he was absolutely terrific-looking and naturally charming. And off-limits?

Pete Morrison should be off-limits. She was completing her study and then getting a job halfway around the world. No reason to get involved. It wasn't logical. She didn't have time for a relationship.

Satisfied he was there to help and she needed to curb her attraction, she slapped her thighs, ready to cooperate. "I have a passport to verify who I am. It's at the observatory housing where I'm staying until I get my telescope time. I'm only here for three weeks."

He put the truck in motion. "So it was just coincidence that you were at the Viewing Area looking for the lights? Tourist or PhD work?"

"Filling in for a student. It's an ongoing study by UT. That's why I was driving her car. I hope her insurance covers accident by strange helicopter. She's going to kill me."

"No comment. I don't let people borrow my truck." He put the patrol car in Drive. "Not even my dad."

The circular building where tourists stopped to watch for the Marfa Lights phenomenon passed by amid several parked vehicles, including another squad car identical to the one she was inside. The radio squawked, and Pete lifted the hand microphone to his lips. It certainly was easy to think of the man by his first name.

"Yeah, Dad?"

"And what if it hadn't been me?" answered a gruff voice through the static.

"It's always you." Pete laughed after he'd released

the talk button and couldn't be heard. "Remember that I have a ride-along."

"I ain't that old, buster Pete. Not much new here, but DHS wants you to meet them at the station with the witness."

"Headed there now. Out."

He stowed the microphone, and she waited for an explanation, but waiting wasn't really her thing. She was more of a straight-to-the-point, fixer type of person and yet she really didn't want to explain right now.

"Real DHS?" she asked, gulping at the potential conversation she'd be forced to have soon.

"The Department of Homeland Security. Looks like our missing body rang some official bells."

"Dang it." *Are they here for a missing body or because of my involvement?* It didn't take much to come to the conclusion it was about her. "Did they mention why they want to talk to me?"

"They probably need your statement. This is a good thing. They'll move the investigation forward a lot faster. You should be glad. We'll be out of your hair that much sooner."

Her instinct and her luck shouted differently.

"Not likely. Why is this happening now? Oh, I know you mentioned the guns and drugs and border thing. But I'm so close to finishing this dissertation. Shoot."

They entered Marfa and turned north toward the

county jail. Pete let his department dispatch know they were on their way in.

"Did they say who would be coming here?" she asked.

"You know someone at Homeland Security?"

Hopefully, she wouldn't have to explain herself. She'd give her interview, they'd say everything was a huge mistake, no one's actually trying to kill you and she could return to finish her short time in the Davis Mountains. "I'd rather not get into it."

"Andrea, you're the one who brought it up."

"And I'm the one who's not going to talk about it." *Not unless I really, really have to.*

Chapter Five

Close to nine in the morning, an official government vehicle pulled in front of the Presidio County Sheriff's Department. One uniformed man got out. Navy, lots of rank. He openly assessed the street, then spent several minutes checking his phone.

Pete watched everything, but his main focus was Andrea. Her posture changed. She looked defeated. After she'd said she didn't want to discuss the DHS, she didn't discuss anything. Gone was the chatty, confident woman who spoke her mind. Now she was withdrawn, closed off, silent, and stood with her hands wrapped around her waist.

The officer acknowledged Pete, but his eyes had connected with Andrea and he wasn't looking anywhere else.

"Commander," Andrea said on a long, exasperated sigh and led the way to his dad's office. She clearly didn't want the DHS representative to be the man who'd walked into the sheriff's office.

"Andrea," the DHS expert acknowledged with

a similar annoyed exhale. He shut the door behind him, leaving only silhouettes against the opaque window—letting Pete know they were on opposite sides of the small room.

Interesting. His witness recognized military rank and the DHS officer seemed to know her. She'd been tight-lipped since they arrived at the station. Either pretending to be asleep on his cot in the back or flat out refusing to answer any questions.

"Do you want something to eat, Pete?" Honey asked.

The shift change had occurred at eight o'clock sharp, just like every normal day. Peach and Honey insisted on working seven days a week, knowing his dad would let them off anytime they wanted. They liked staying busy, but they liked staying out of each other's hair more. They'd each confided in him—and probably everyone else in town—that it was the only reason they continued to live in the same house.

"No, thanks, Honey. I thought I'd take Miss Allen to the café when she's done."

"Are you sure she's not going to be whisked away by aliens or a secret government agency?" The older woman laughed, making fun of several theories Peach had shared before leaving. "The sheriff is hung up at the scene for at least another hour, Pete. He wanted me to let you know."

He could guess why his father hadn't spoken to

him directly. Most likely to keep his cool at the lack of cooperation. "He still fighting for information?"

"I can only assume so," Honey said, picking up her pen. "You know those government types. They never let us in on the fun."

"You adding this to your novel?" he asked, and was ignored since she was already engrossed in writing her sentence.

Peach came up with the stories and Honey was the aspiring writer who wrote them down. They'd kept the local women busy debating the realism of their tales for several years. It was obvious even to strangers that they were best friends who happened to be sisters.

A yawn escaped him. It was the first double shift he'd completed without a wink of shut-eye in a long while. But he couldn't head back to the ranch until DHS instructed them on what was to happen with Andrea. His dad would be at the scene awhile. That left him with nothing to do but catch up on paperwork and wait for their guests to finish. He'd be lucky if he could go home afterward.

"Since things are covered at the moment, I'm going to grab a quick shower in the back and wake up. Alert me if they," he said, hooking his thumb toward his dad's closed office door, "finish up."

"I have a feeling they're going to be there awhile," Honey said. "Don't you think it's a bit strange that he's here to interview a witness and didn't even introduce himself?"

"I suppose you have a point. I'm not certain what protocol is for something like this. We normally don't share murder jurisdiction with anyone."

"You certain there's not going to be another murder soon?"

Voices were definitely rising on the other side of the window, but the old building had walls thick enough that he couldn't distinguish the words. Should he step inside and allow them to cool off? If he was closer, maybe he could understand what the argument was about.

"Do you think you should join them and referee?" Honey asked.

Pete took definite steps toward the arguing and stopped. It only took those three steps to realize he'd been waiting on encouragement from Honey so he could barge in and rescue Andrea again.

Son of a gun.

He was more interested in this fascinating woman than the murder and the disappearing body. He pivoted and headed into the back.

"Ten minutes. That's all I need for a shower."

"*I* could eavesdrop?"

"Get back to your writing, Honey."

"Yes, sir."

The door slamming had nothing to do with his actions. They'd been meaning to fix the mechanism that slowed the heavy door from crashing shut. He hadn't thought about it until the loud crash echoed in the concrete hallway. He threw his stuff into the locker and jumped under an icy spray, not giving the water time to warm.

Holding cells and the jail were on a different floor. He needed to put some effort into this case. His thoughts were centered more on Andrea's relationship with Homeland Security than getting his notes together for the investigation or why someone would steal the body of a dead man.

He'd offered to try to identify the missing man but had been specifically instructed not to even print pictures from the camera. Normally, he hated being shut out and treated like a wet-behind-the-ears rookie. Today, it had hardly crossed his mind. But it had, and soon after, he'd copied the pictures to a memory stick and stuck it in his pocket.

On the flip side, he couldn't *stop* thinking about Andrea Allen. He had no reason to book her and no criminal record he could find. DHS had just asked her to be held until they arrived.

Who was she? Where was she going after the observatory? What was her life like? Where had she been? How had she gotten that jagged old scar under her chin and the small one just above her collarbone?

Three weeks wasn't a long time to get the answers. Might be even less time. She'd mentioned three weeks total but had never mentioned how long she'd been here.

Pete toweled off and stuck his legs in his pants as quickly as a surprised rattler about to strike. He wasn't about to miss the opportunity to speak with the officer when he left. He considered shaving, but it would take too much time.

Looking in the mirror one last time, he shoved his hair straight back and caught movement behind him. His weapon was still secure in his locker, so he spun, ready for—

"Andrea? How'd you get back here? I didn't hear the door."

"Some of us know how to close one without slamming it. They probably heard you come through it on Proxima Centauri."

"Prox what?" He leaned against the sink, crossing his arms and just enjoying how she could look so dang sexy even in teddy bear scrubs. The meek, insecure side of the woman he'd been admiring was gone. Spunky, speak-your-mind PhD candidate was approaching him one sure step at a time.

"It's the nearest star to earth, with the exception of our sun, of course. But it's not my favorite."

"The sun? I'm sort of fond of it."

"As I can see by your tan. No, Proxima Centauri. It's such a stuffy name."

She halted within arm's distance. A dangerous distance. Close enough to see his attraction reflected in her soft blue eyes. The desire to put a hand on each of her hips and draw her to him was tremendous. He had to clear his throat to think of something other than the pink lacy bra he'd seen earlier.

"I should go speak with the DHS officer." He took a step to move past her and ended with a slender hand on his chest.

"The Commander's gone to the scene. He said to stay put until he returned. Looks like you're stuck with me, Sheriff Morrison."

"*Acting* sheriff. Why don't you call me Pete." Was he insulted? Or too dang excited he didn't need to dart off to talk shop? *Excited.*

"I need to show you something."

"I don't think that's appropriate."

She threw back her head, laughing. He barely heard it as he admired the bend of her neck. "Silly. Do you have any gel?"

"Huh?" *Silly* wasn't the word filtering through his mind.

"Styling gel."

"I used it already."

"Not enough to do anything." She reached around him, brushing his arm as she squeezed goo into her hands.

Stunned into silence? Choking on his words? Cat got his tongue? He didn't know which, and if she asked, he couldn't hear her. He was focused on her hands rubbing together and then her arms lifting to reach his head.

"Get shorter." She tapped the inside of his bare feet wider apart, leaving enough room between them to breathe without touching.

"So, what *is* your favorite star?" he asked, closing his eyes and enjoying her fingers lightly massaging his scalp as she liberally put gel on every strand. He couldn't look.

"Wolf 359. Isn't that an awesome name for a star?" She took the tube a second time. "Just a bit more. Your hair's really thick and wavy."

He was dang lucky he'd put his pants on quickly. If he hadn't…

"See?"

All he could see was the roundness of each breast under the thin layer of hospital garb.

"All you have to do is squeeze some on your hands and rub it around like this. Then it should stay looking deliberately messed up all day." She wiped her hands on his towel and admired her handiwork. "That will look much better later when it's dry."

She twisted one last piece of hair and placed her hands on his shoulders. It seemed like the most natural gesture in his memory for his fingers to move and span either side of her waist. Drawing her closer to him was just as easy.

They were forehead to forehead. Her slow, warm exhale smelled sweet like the cola she'd insisted on before the officer had arrived. She'd called it her wake-up drink of choice. He, on the other hand, loved coffee and lots of it.

Concentrate on the job. What job? All he had to do was hang around here, keep her in sight till she was someone else's problem. Maybe even escort her home.

"I'm not a rule breaker, Andrea."

"Then why are your hands still around me?"

Kissing her was destined as soon as she'd told him they'd never get along. "What's about to happen probably shouldn't. But you won't find me apologizing for it later."

"You better not, Pete. Bad first kissers don't get a second chance."

He liked her. A lot. Too much. Too fast.

He leaned his lips to touch hers for the first time. Soft and wet, they parted just enough to encourage him. His hands spread up her back, noticing the firm muscles.

There wasn't anything between them now except a thin layer of cotton. He stopped himself from getting the shirt out of his way. This was their first kiss but sure didn't feel like it.

Their lips slid together, teasing, seeming to know their way without conscious effort. A perfect fit? Practiced. Confident.

He wanted his hands to wander but forced them to stay put. Andrea's arms encircled his neck, shifting her body next to his. Her tennis shoes snuggled next to his size-thirteen feet. That one layer kept him both sane and drove him crazy at the same time.

He wanted it off. Wanted her bare skin under his

flesh. Wanted to forget exactly where they were and remember everything much too late.

The attraction turned to mutual pure hunger and he liked her even more.

Chapter Six

Maybe it was defying her father, the Commander. Maybe it was a bit of the rebellious daughter in her that forced the need to push him at every turn. Or maybe she saw something in this man that she recognized as rare. A part of him that was wise beyond his years.

Attraction or defiance. It didn't matter for Andrea. Not at this moment. She was totally enthralled by Pete's kissing abilities. Something she hadn't experienced in a long time, if ever.

"Did I pass?" he asked when they came up for air, continuing small kisses and nips down her neck.

"I think you've earned a second audition." She tilted her head back to give him better access.

A few light touches of those incredible lips across her shoulder where the large scrubs top fell to the side and then he stood straight. She was close enough to notice the tiny gold flecks in his dark brown eyes. Hard chest, hard shoulders, hard biceps. This man was all man, yet playful. And those dimples were just killer.

She liked him. He was perfect for her plan to ignore her father.

"And just when is this second audition to take place?" he asked, his voice rich with the desire displayed in his eyes.

"How long does it take to get back to the observatory?" She had to entice him into taking her home.

"I thought you were ordered to stay put?" His hands slid under her loose top, warming her bare back and exposing her belly as the top inched higher.

"Technically, but I'd be safe with you. We came to an understanding." She did a little of her own exploring, dragging her nails across his well-sculpted muscles.

"I think you may have gotten the wrong impression about me." He gently circled her wrists with his fingers and returned their hands to their sides.

"Why do you say that?" Andrea painted the words with innocence.

He took a couple of steps backward and opened the door. "Honey?"

"Yes, Pete?"

"Did the Commander leave any parting words?"

"You mean when he said, 'I expect my daughter to be here when I return'? That's pretty much everything."

When Pete smiled a really healthy smile that made it all the way to his eyes, he had dimpled cheeks to match the one in his chin. She truly was a sucker for dimples. He let the door close, crossed his arms and leaned that bare back against the gray paint. "So he's your father. How did you understand those specific instructions to include a drive up the mountain?"

"Are you going to let him order you around? You aren't in the Navy. Technically, he doesn't have any jurisdiction. He's only here because I'm involved." Her dad was assigned to the Customs and Border Protection Office, reporting directly to the DHS. He had every right to ask the local sheriff for cooperation in a case. But he hadn't. And forcing her to stay at the county jail wasn't about any case. It was about controlling her life.

"To use a word you seem to love—*technically* he's with Homeland Security. I haven't been filled in yet, but he does have some authority around here. Your dad wants you to stay put and be safe. My dad wants me to stay put and see that you are." He pushed off the door, twisted the combination on a lock and lifted the latch of a locker. He pulled out a crisply starched uniform shirt and shoved his hands through the sleeves.

"Your jerky movements may be revealing your true feelings. Or they could be showing me your true nature."

"Maybe I just failed the second audition." After turning his back, he pushed the tail of his shirt inside his pants.

"I know my rights. You can't keep me here against my will. You certainly can't use the excuse *her daddy made me do it*. It will all be on you when I sue the county."

"At the moment, I'm too tired to care. I've gone without sleep for a couple of nights and haven't had the privilege of napping like you. So let me spell this out real plain like. You have two choices. Spend your time here in protective custody locked in a cell or walk down the street and have breakfast with me. Simple. You choose."

"You won't change your mind about that audition?" She added a wink, teasing him.

"I'm too hungry to change my mind." He stretched his neck, swiveling his head from side to side.

She made a grand gesture to follow him. "Lead on."

"Be right there. I walk better in my boots."

If she could get through the door before he buckled his gun around his hips, she might have enough of a head start to ditch the impromptu bodyguard her father had assigned. Then what? Downtown wasn't filled with public transportation and there certainly wasn't a taxi waiting on the corner.

The heavy door to the restricted area slammed behind her. She'd at least wait in the comfy chair in his office. Getting far away from his dimples seemed a good idea. The more he smiled at her, the more she was willing to change the venue of his *audition*.

Who was she trying to fool? Pete had already passed any audition with flying colors. She had one more Saturday night in West Texas and hoped this was the last time she thought about being bored.

Before she could sit, the restricted door slammed again. Pete scooted through, one boot on and one boot in his hand. With the office door open, she could watch his head turn, searching and landing on the receptionist.

He looked straight at her, let out a deep breath, showing his relief, and pulled on his second boot. "Good. I'm too tired to run."

"Don't get comfortable. There's been a disturbance near Doug Fossen's place. A burning vehicle on the side of the road near the state park."

"That's Davis County jurisdiction. Give Mike Barber a call."

"They know that but think you need to see it."

"Send Griggs, then."

"He hasn't reported in this morning and they're asking for the sheriff. That's you."

"What the..." He took a piece of paper from the woman. She looked a lot like the receptionist who had been at the front desk when they arrived. "Honey, please call Peach and see if she forgot to give me a message about Griggs."

"Pete, you know she didn't forget. I can get Joe to write Griggs up if you don't want to do it. But right now we have a problem at the Fossens'."

"I have babysitting duty."

Andrea stuck her head out the office door. "Don't mind this baby. I can sleep in that nice jail cell you suggested. I'm sure the Commander would prefer me safe and sound, guarded by a senior citizen." She nodded toward the receptionist. "No offense."

"None taken," Honey said, bringing the ringing handset up to her ear. "Presidio County Sheriff's Department." Honey wrote more notes. "We'll get someone out there shortly, Mrs. Fossen." She waved the slips in the air.

"I'm not heading anywhere, Honey. I smell a mess brewing and there's no way I'm taking anyone with me on a call." Pete reached for his hat on a nearby desk. He almost shoved his hair off his forehead. He stopped, tapped the styling gel now hardened in place and then scratched the bridge of his nose.

"Sounds like you need to get a move on." She raised her wrists to him. "Do your duty, Sheriff Pete. Lock me away."

His moment of indecision played on his handsome face. Then it was chased away with confidence. "Honey, get my dad or somebody from the accident last night on the radio."

"Yes, sir," the receptionist said.

"I'm not doing it. Send Dominguez and Hardy." He muttered something under his breath. "Come on, Andrea."

"Mind if I take the jacket from your office?"

"It's not my office, but I'm sure the sheriff won't mind."

With Honey answering the ringing phone and Pete rubbing the bridge of his nose, she walked to the coatrack in the corner. All the framed pictures on the wall were of Pete growing up. There was no mistaking the cleft in his chin or the tall, lanky frame. They were snapshots from his life of sports, school and graduation. One caught him shoving his hand through his hair and setting his hat on his head.

"That one's my favorite. He looks so uncomplicated, don't you think?" Honey stood in the doorway, arms crossed over her Davis Mountains souvenir T-shirt.

"I imagine he's rarely uncomplicated."

"You're a smart woman for picking up on that so quickly. He went for breakfast or he's using you as the excuse to fill his belly. We didn't get to officially meet earlier. I'm Honey, part-time dispatcher and unofficial receptionist around here. You met my sister, Peach, when you arrived earlier."

"You look alike."

"Don't tell her that." Honey laughed. "Do you have everything you need?"

"Yes, thanks. Sorry if the Commander offended you earlier. I wish I could say he was stressed and this wasn't his usual behavior, but today is just business as usual. I love him, but sometimes he's rather rude."

"I totally understand, sweetie. I hope you like breakfast burritos. That's just about all Pete ever has time to grab from that café." Honey crossed her arms over her heaving bosom and planted herself in the middle of the doorway.

"Anything's fine. Some of these pictures are really good. Have you known them long?" She quickly received the message that Pete had gone to the café alone and she was staying put. She might as well glean useful information about her adversary.

"Pete's worked with his dad since he was— Actually, I can't remember a time Pete wasn't here in this office. The sheriff prior to Joe paid him to empty the trash and sweep up as soon as he could hold a broom."

"Was his mom behind the camera in all these?" Andrea pointed at the wall, noticing that there weren't any with women.

"No. One of Pete's parents was a second cousin or something to Joe. They died and Pete came to live in Marfa. Poor man never considered marrying, but adopted a three-year-old without missing a beat. Peach and I moved here close to the same time."

"I'm glad Pete found someone and things worked out for him. And thanks. I would have really stepped in it asking about his mom if you hadn't shared."

"The whole community's been contributing to that wall. He's like one of our own, you know."

"I sure didn't want to spend all morning locked in that cell. Maybe we should go back to your desk." She got close enough to hug Honey—even though that was the furthest thing from her mind. She gestured to move out of the room, and then it hit her. "I get it. You're supposed to watch me until Pete gets back. Aren't you?"

Honey smiled, crossing her arms and planting her large frame in the doorway. "He reminded me that it's part of my job responsibilities designated under 'other.' I offered to get his breakfast, but he said he needed a break. Sorry, but you aren't going anywhere until Pete comes for you. He's smarter than he is cute."

"Ha, he is pretty darn cute. This doesn't have anything to do with him. Not really. I'll lose two years of work if I'm here when the Commander comes back. He'll haul me to Austin or worse, DC. I'll be unable to finish my thesis and..." Trying to talk her way out of the office wasn't working. "You don't care one rogue meteor what this is going to do to my life."

This couldn't be happening. She only needed six more days.

"Take a seat, Miss Allen." Honey crossed her arms and stood as straight as her aged body would allow. "I do know that *caring* about prisoners is not in my job description."

For a split second she considered making a run for it out the restricted door through the back exit.

But there was nowhere for her to go. Staying with Pete wasn't a bad idea. He was the only one who could solve her current problem. She had to avoid her father and stay in West Texas for at least six more days.

Chapter Seven

"I can't be here when my father comes for me."

"You won't be. Let's go." Pete waited for Andrea to follow, cell phone still to his ear.

"Some days are busier than others. Enjoy your ride." Honey answered her ringing phone.

He escorted Andrea to the Tahoe without any instruction. She hopped in and quickly dropped her head against the headrest, closing her eyes and looking completely relaxed.

Pete knew different. He recognized the compliance she thought was necessary until she could talk herself into a different position.

Pete tapped his smartphone and left another message for his dad. "We didn't finish our conversation. Be prepared. I'm dropping Miss Allen off with her father and returning with you. I will lock you up to make you rest. Honey's plumping the pillows in the holding for you. No scene or I swear you won't like being cuffed and thrown into the backseat of your old service vehicle."

He disconnected, debating the logic of moving his witness. She was safer here, in a building filled with law enforcement officers. Yet Commander Allen had been adamant when they spoke. His daughter would be brought to him at the Viewing Area immediately. A chopper was on its way to airlift them home. The directive had included instructions not to inform Andrea where they were heading or why.

Prisoners were kept better informed than this guy treated his daughter.

"When did he call?" Andrea asked as soon as he sat behind the wheel. Questioning arched brows, innocent open eyes and an impish suggestive grin—she looked totally in control.

"Who?" That wouldn't fly. She knew that *he* knew who she was talking about.

"The Commander. I've seen the look of having to swallow his orders many times."

"What you witnessed was me leaving a message for my dad."

"Oh." She looked at him and then her chin went up a notch with her aha moment. "You aren't denying that the Commander called."

"No, I'm not. Why do you call him Commander?"

"I've always addressed him by his rank. Well, at least since I was a teenager. It was easier. He answered to it faster when we were in a crowd and he's never seemed to mind. Since you aren't sharing our destination, I suppose he told you not to tell me. Afraid I'd pitch a fit or something?"

"He didn't mention fits of any sort. In fact, he didn't explain his reasoning with me at all. He seems very concerned about your safety. Why is that exactly?" It had to be finding that man from the desert. Whoever he escaped from—that didn't take a genius to determine—knew he'd made contact with Andrea and they thought she knew something. Including her father.

"I don't know what you mean. I spent all of five minutes in his presence. How does that make him appear concerned?"

"We can skip all the tippytoeing around." He took another look behind them and yet another along the horizon, searching for he didn't know what. "Your father asked me to bring you to the accident site. I disagreed. If men are after you, then you're much more vulnerable alone with me in this vehicle. Doesn't matter that it's only nine miles to their location."

"Did he mention why he wants me there?"

"To leave."

Either Andrea had seen or heard something from her passenger or these men were so well connected they knew she was the daughter of the man investigating them. That would account for a DHS impostor trying to remove her from the hospital.

Her fingers curled into her palms. "I've said this before, but I'm an adult and he has no right—"

"Pete?" Honey's shaky voice broke through on the radio. "Pete, are you there?"

He could tell she was upset. "What's wrong?"

"Jeff Davis County just called. They found our missing deputy's car abandoned near the state park. You want me to send one of the new guys to check it out?"

"Negative. Ask Hardy to head over." He released the button on the microphone.

"You need to go and I'm in the way," Andrea said. "You can drop me off with Honey. I promise to be good."

He pulled the car to the side of the road. "The Viewing Area is still three or four miles. I could drop you off, then hightail it back north."

"Or?"

Something hadn't been sitting right about the facts in this case. Too many coincidences. Too many orders issued. Too many gut feelings that he needed to be doing something active instead of reactive.

"Did I lose you, Pete?" Honey asked.

He spun the vehicle around and brought the microphone up to his mouth. "I'm here. Tell Jeff Davis County I'm on my way and ask if they can wait to move anything."

"That's what they wanted to hear, Pete. They're searching for our deputy as we speak." The radio clicked off and back on. "You still babysitting?"

Andrea rolled her eyes and shook her head. A laugh escaped as he answered, "That's an affirmative."

Honey laughed into the microphone. "Think they'll find our deputy passed out on a park bench?"

"I'll write the reprimand myself. On my way."

Pete's rash decision about bringing a witness to a crime scene would come back and bite him. He was certain about that. He was also certain she'd done her best to manipulate him with the make-out session and talk about second auditions. Andrea Allen sat next to him because *she* wanted to be there. She might have just hypnotized him or something with those large, dark blue eyes. Yep, this decision would definitely bite him in the end.

"I never stood a chance," he mumbled aloud.

"Did you say something?"

"Yeah, stay in the car when we arrive until I give you permission to get out. Or I'll put you in cuffs for your own protection."

"Sure thing. That was a good breakfast burrito."

Was she agreeing just a little too quickly? Changing the subject even quicker? If she wanted it changed, he could roll with that.

"Always is from the café. I'm thinking you should tell me what's going on between you and your dad. Why are you afraid he's going to take you home? You're a little old for a runaway."

"That's funny, but not far from the truth. I've been running from my parents since I was twenty and wanted to change my major the first time."

"You've changed more than once?"

"Not really. I let them talk me into completing three."

"So you're an overachiever. Will this be a fourth?"

"Not an overachiever as much as… Well, I feel more like a compliant child. I'm working on my doctorate in space studies and need to be here to finish up."

"Sounds like a complicated relationship."

"You know how parents and college are," she said casually.

"Not really." He repeated her words, wanting to avoid his life history as much as possible.

"You didn't have to go to become a police officer?" She looked genuinely confused. "You're looking at me like I'm a cat with two heads."

"My dad has been sheriff in this county since I graduated from high school. He was a deputy before that. I've been around that office my entire life. I didn't need any references or education except what he could teach me."

"Is this all you ever want to do? Be sheriff?"

"You say that like it's a bad thing."

"No, I'm sorry. I always have an uncanny ability to say exactly what makes people uncomfortable or just end up insulting them."

"Well, now that you mention it…"

"Seriously, I apologize. I just meant…is being sheriff your dream or your father's?"

"Both, I guess. I haven't ever given it much thought. Everyone just assumed I would be."

He hadn't given it much thought until his dad's heart attack and he'd been asked to step in. It was always one day in a future he assumed was way down the road. Now? His father's bombshell had exploded and was a constant distraction.

He couldn't dwell on that problem. Andrea was enough distraction for any man to handle.

"Not too many people have wanted the job. It's a lot of territory and a lot of nothing. It's just so excitin' and all."

"Now you're just teasing. You've had alien visitors, a missing body, an attempted homicide and Homeland Security taking over an investigation all in less than twelve hours. I am very confident that everyone wants to be in your shoes." Andrea smiled, teasing him at every turn.

"Yeah, I see what you mean." He did have a decision to make about the election. Soon. But not before he needed to find a missing deputy and determine what was really going on in his county. And if he let this woman go before he had some basic questions answered, they might go unanswered for quite a long while.

He drove. Quickly, efficiently. He knew every shortcut not only in his county, but also to the north and east.

"I've always been told I'd achieve certain things. There are only problems when I assume I can go about them in my own fashion..." Her voice drifted off and she looked out the window.

"Sheriff, this is Honey. Where are you?"

He picked up the car radio. "About three miles south of Fort Davis."

"They found Logan."

He heard the shakiness to her voice. She wasn't irritated—a tone he'd heard plenty of times from her being interrupted. She'd been crying. "What aren't you saying?"

"It's not good, Pete."

"Are you talking about Logan Griggs?" Andrea asked, gripping his arm.

He nodded. "Why? Do you know him?"

"That's Sharon's boyfriend. She's the woman I was covering for last night. They had a date. Do you— Do you think…?"

He knew what she didn't want to ask. If they'd been returning from Alpine and were stopped by the same men who had tried to kill her…

"Both of your fathers are headed there now. Should I tell them you're on your way?"

"Negative. They'll find out soon enough. Inform the searchers there may be a woman missing."

"Come again?"

"A UT student may have been with Griggs. Tell them and keep me posted."

What a mess.

"Before you try to convince me to take you someplace other than to meet your father, we need to stop the secretiveness."

"Absolutely. Do you really think Sharon was with him?"

"There's more to your accident than you're telling me. Homeland doesn't send teams to investigate car accidents for six hours. Not even when daughters are involved. Now, what's going on?"

"I…I swear I don't know. Sharon asked me to cover for her at the last minute. That's all. She had a date, didn't want to watch for the lights, asked me to take pictures if anything happened and even let me borrow her car." She raised fingers as she went through her mental list.

"Did you take pictures?" That had to be what they were after. "Where is the camera? I didn't find one in the car."

"I…I dropped it in the front seat when I dragged the man into the back. It had to be in the car. Do you think it got thrown out during the crash?"

"I made a cursory search in the dark, then followed your tracks and took you to the hospital."

"Then those men followed you to the hospital."

Pete turned the Tahoe into the state park entrance, eager to confirm that this accident was connected to the other. Dreading the sight of one of his deputies—and friend—being the victim of a homicide. Dreading more that he knew it wasn't an accident and that he needed to warn the woman next to him.

"Andrea, as more information comes to light, I have a gnawing feeling that none of this has been coincidence. I don't think anyone followed me to the hospital. I think they were prepared for the possibility you might get away. That they expected you to be at the Viewing Area last night."

She stared at her hands, shaking her head in disbelief. "No way."

"Do you think they could be setting a trap to get rid of your father? Has anything like this ever happened before?"

"He's only been DHS for a year or so, but no. Never."

"You're staying with me. I'm responsible for you. You will listen to me, understand? I tell you to stay in the car, you stay in the car. I tell you to do anything, you do it. Got it?"

A man had tried to abduct her, had knocked her across the room just hours ago and she hadn't looked as worried as right now, staring at him.

"You can't be right about this, Pete. But even if you aren't, you're beginning to scare me a little."

"Well, damn. I meant to scare you a lot."

Chapter Eight

Andrea waited in the car as instructed. Not because Pete had sworn her to obedience or issued orders. If waiting in the car hadn't been the safest place physically, it was the safest place mentally. Logan's body had been found not far from the car on the other side of the hill.

The car fire had brought the park rangers to the main road. They'd extinguished the dry brush before it had gotten out of control about the time she and Pete arrived. She'd put her face in her hands and refused to watch after Pete parked. She didn't want the image of a wrecked car, possibly with charred bodies, forever in her memory. The fake ones in movies were bad enough to fuel her imagination.

The sunlight began chasing shadows away at the bottom of the nearby hills where officers searched for evidence. And for Sharon, who hadn't returned to the observatory housing last night.

Plain, simple, old-fashioned apprehension had her short, practical nails digging into her palms. It built in her chest, clogging her throat until she wanted to jump from the SUV. She pushed the door open and was greeted by the horrible acrid smell of burning plastic. Dark smoke continued to billow into the sparse trees.

The guilt and uncertainty of what she should do played with her mind. Pete had scared her with his declaration before jumping out of the truck to identify Logan's body.

Was she in danger if she stayed to finish her study? She swiped the tears trickling down her face. Sharon had been so full of life…

Had her young coworker died because those monsters thought it had been Pete returning her to the observatory? Was this her fault? What was she supposed to do now? Or had Sharon set her up to be kidnapped so they could manipulate the Commander?

After what they'd been through at the hospital, she trusted Pete to defend her and do it well. She respected his honesty along with his ability. She also appreciated that he wasn't bossing her around because he could. He had every right, and he could have left her in a jail cell waiting on the Commander. She knew what her father would do. A decree would be made and if she didn't follow his instructions to the letter, an agent or officer she didn't know would enforce his orders.

Parents shouldn't have that type of authority over their twenty-six-year-old children. Especially since she'd been paying her own way since her first degree. And most didn't. She was the only person who gave her parents the authority. This was her life, but she had the feeling it was about to spin completely out of her control.

Six days was all she needed to finish her dissertation and get the dream job halfway around the world. Far away from Commander Tony Allen, former astronaut now working for the Department of Homeland Security. And farther away from Dr. Beatrice Allen, wife, perfect mother and foremost authority on the Brontë sisters in the United States.

Even with three degrees behind her, Andrea felt compelled to argue for a thesis on a once-in-a-lifetime star. She'd fought for her allotted time tracking it over the next week. Even though the observatory had been perfectly willing to record what the telescope found and send it to her, she'd insisted on being here. Personally overseeing the collection of data, trying to impress experts halfway around the world.

If she failed…what then? Another degree? In another subject? Another direction? Give in and teach with her mother? Hear all the reasons she'd failed because she'd chosen a terrible topic or that she must not have applied herself enough?

Her parents' voices saying "I told you so" rang through her head. They'd been right too many times to ignore.

This was her last shot. One star was certain to

rise over the next six days. The question was if she'd watch it from behind an international telescope or if she'd see it on TV designated by her father as secure.

Pete tapped on the driver's window, and she unlocked the doors. "No, she's with me and staying with me. Especially now." He carefully set his hat in the backseat, kept the phone to his ear and made a motion for the keys.

While he was gone, she'd kept them in her hand. She placed the key in the ignition and started the car. Pete looked at her strangely and agreed with whomever he was talking to. Cell still to his ear, he put the car in gear and took off quickly, a cloud of dust billowing behind them.

"Two males. About a hundred yards from the vehicle. No, that's not in question." He paused, listening. "No, she's not staying. I agree, not over the phone. I assume someone's listening and I won't risk it."

"What's not a problem?" she asked, but he hadn't hung up and just waved her question aside.

"Yes, sir. I understand, sir." Pete stuck the phone in his shirt pocket.

"I can tell that was my father. What are our orders now?"

"Your transport is meeting us at the observatory."

"And I have no say in it." She wanted to fight for her right to stay and yet…two men were dead.

"No, Andrea, you don't. It's obvious to everyone now that *you* were the target. The man beside Griggs in that ditch is the same one from the car."

"And Sharon?" She'd barely known the young woman, but her heart sank under the guilt. Sharon was probably dead because Pete had taken her to Marfa instead of to the observatory. If it hadn't been for Pete finding her when he did, she'd be dead, too.

Pete's phone rang, squealing a hard-rock tune she loved before he tapped it and raised it to his ear. "Come on, Dad. Take it easy on the man and work with him. Right. You, too. See you at the ranch."

Question after question rammed their way into her mind and needed to be asked as soon as Pete set the phone down.

"They thought they were us. That could have been you. Oh, my God, I can't believe— I mean, I know what that suit tried to do last night, but it all sort of seemed surreal. You were there to stop him. What do we do now? I mean, I heard what you said, but are you taking me to the Commander? He's going to ship me home on the first plane headed in that direction. Or any direction, for that matter."

"Honestly, Andrea, you throw out so many questions that I don't know where to start. They haven't found your friend. Were you close?"

"Not really. I just can't believe she's dead."

"The body from last night is an undercover agent working for your father." His grip tightened on the wheel. He was obviously upset, too. "I'll wait with you until your father's helicopter arrives. He's ordered—"

"I'm not leaving."

"Someone's trying to kill you. Two people are dead, maybe three. What do you mean you aren't going?"

"I've waited two years for this one week. This one specific week. I'm scheduled to use the telescope for the next six nights. If I don't, all of my research is useless."

"And that's more important than your life?"

"I have one shot at this star."

"In the right wind, one shot's all any sniper needs."

"You really believe that my life is in danger?"

"Yes. Or worse," he mumbled, but she heard him loud and clear.

"Then I'll go." She really had no choice. The longer she stayed here, the more people she put in danger. Her father had loosely warned about threats a year ago when he was transferred. Until that very moment, she'd never believed anyone would actually threaten her.

Now she was indirectly responsible for at least one man dying. She couldn't handle another—specifically Pete—losing his life, too.

"You're not just saying the words that I want to hear. You're going to leave when the time comes?" He reached out and tipped her chin upward. Her eyes raised from her hands and focused on the dimples apparent in his cheeks.

His smile relieved the apprehension, lessened the guilt, made her want to spar with him again. "Do you need me to pinkie-swear or something, Sheriff?"

"Acting sheriff, and no." He rested the crook of his arm on the back of the seat between them. "So... um...I guess this will be it. I don't suppose you'll be back for another look at the stars anytime soon. I was sort of looking forward to that second audition."

"Yeah, me, too."

Chapter Nine

"If you know where this woman will be, why not just let the men shoot to kill?" Patrice Orlando strummed her extra-long nails against each other in a ghastly rhythm. "Homeland Security will surely bring in extra patrols we'll need to avoid."

"I'd like to find out what she knows before we disrupt months of planning." He disliked repeating himself, especially to the same person.

He moved around his library, passing the multiple chessboards along one wall. If Patrice would satisfy her thirst—either for his wine or her delusion that she had any part in the decision making of this operation—he could achieve checkmate in three moves with board four. He contemplated his next play on chessboard one.

"But Homeland is involved now," she whined.

He hated whiners, but she was necessary for a major component of his plan.

"Yes, it does present a challenge that needs a

complex solution. And yet I've dealt with complicated problems before, if you recall."

"Not like this."

"My dear, why do you continually doubt my ability? Didn't you say that the last time we faced an
adversary?"

"Getting rid of two Texas Rangers is not the same
as the Department of Homeland Security. Why
would they send a man undercover into our operation, anyway?"

Explaining oneself was the tedious part of working with expendable assets. Yet sometimes it was
necessary to ease their minds and clue them in to
the big picture, as someone once reminded him.
He might be able to see several moves ahead, but
he did have a propensity to forget others could not.

"I'll begin with your question. One small re-
minder, Patrice, that Homeland is in charge of our
borders. We have outwitted them on several occa-
sions regarding our gun trade. And we are a major
drug supplier in the south. Soon to be number one,
I might add. Therefore, it makes perfect sense for
DHS to weasel an operative into our business."

"Can't you stop talking down to me, Mr. Rook? I
get all that. I'm not a dummy." Patrice guzzled the
remainder of the California pinot noir.

She might not be a "dummy" about certain com-
ponents of their business dealings, but when it came
to wine, she needed a great deal of schooling. After

four years of her visits, he didn't bother any longer. "I meant no offense, dear."

"Just spell it out. We've been lucky. I just want to keep that trend trending."

Luck? Dozens of plans had been considered and one had been carefully chosen, then manipulated into action. There had been no *luck* involved.

"The Texas Rangers were out of the picture for almost four years because of one of my simple plans, as you referred to it." He sat at board number two, wanting the intricately carved pieces to fill his vision instead of Patrice's continual pacing around the room. "Once they reappeared, they were distracted with their wild-goose chase. Patrice, come sit down."

"We're wasting our time and resources. I don't want anything to go wrong. What's the point of capturing this woman who happened to see the crew last night? Don't we already know she switched at the last minute?"

"Patrice, Patrice, Patrice." He rose and placed his hands on her shoulders, patting them like a pet dog.

He'd never had a dog. He couldn't abide the shedding, drooling or constant neediness. He'd tried a cat once, but soon disposed of it. He supposed the people who worked for him were pets enough, but he preferred to think of them all as pawns.

"Why can't you appreciate the fine chessboard that I've set into motion? This is the part I enjoy."

"Chess has never been my thing." She smiled

uncomfortably. He saw her reaction in one of the many mirrors he had strategically placed around the room for just this occasion.

"And still you've accomplished so many aspects of a refined chessman," he complimented her, forcing the words he barely could say, squeezing her shoulders a bit. Patrice was far from a disciplined chess player. "You are very good at guile, manipulation and distraction. Dispatch four of your best, dear. I want this accomplished this morning."

"Four of my best?"

"If you want to achieve your goal, then you must be willing to sacrifice your players." He moved his queen's bishop, knowing the piece would be captured. He'd left his opponent no choice. The sacrifice would be seen as a potential deadly mistake, but in the long run it would help him achieve his goal of checkmate.

"That…that…hurts—"

"They are easily replaced. More can be trained."

He applied even more pressure, certain her skin would be bruised the next time he saw it.

To her triumph, she didn't pout or ask him to stop. "Where should she be taken?"

"I will make the arrangements. Notify me when the deed is done." He released the pressure and petted the bruised flesh.

"Yes, sir." She carefully wiped a tear from the corner of her eye.

Pain could remind pawns faster than any words.

"We shall give the authorities another bone to dig their teeth into for a while. It appeases the American taxpayers and we go on our merry way for some time before they drag their hungry behinds back to the border for more."

"And what is this bone?"

"Andrea Allen."

Chapter Ten

Andrea's bags were packed and would be shipped later. Her laptop and change of clothes were in her shoulder bag. She looked around the observatory with a feeling of desolation. Everyone around her was determined she'd leave on that helicopter with her dad and...

That was the problem. There was no "and." If she left the McDonald Observatory and her research, there wasn't an option left for her. Nothing except a second-rate teaching job at a university already overstaffed with more than enough astronomers twiddling their thumbs. Well, it might not be that horrible.

But it wasn't her dream job. Nor did it sound exciting at all. Definitely not as exciting as working in Germany, Australia or South Africa.

"You don't look too happy."

"You think?" she smarted off to her rescuer turned guard. "I'm sorry, Pete. It's just that my dad is so overprotective. Because of his position and authority, everyone just falls into line with any decision, complying with his every wish."

"Got it."

Sheriff Morrison opened his stance and placed himself back to the wall, facing the entrance, staring straight ahead. Straight over her head. He probably didn't realize his hands rested on his belt, his right very near the hilt of his pistol. He was ready for whatever might come their way.

It was just plain selfish of her not to acknowledge the risk he was taking or the friend he'd just lost.

"I'm sorry, I realize you'd rather be investigating your friend's death."

"My job's right here." He continued his guard duty, never meeting her eyes, looking anywhere—everywhere—but at her.

"Forget it. I'm not running away. I know I have to leave. I can't let anyone else get hurt because of me." *Or murdered.* She saw the words on his face with the minuscule clenching of his jaw. "I appreciate you staying with me until the Commander arrives."

"I gave my word," he said matter-of-factly, without much inflection or a shrug. He looked like every soldier who had ever stood guard over her growing up.

"Of course you did. I'm appreciative nonetheless." Not only did he look the same as those soldiers, he acted the same, too. "They should be here any minute. I think I'll wait outside."

"I don't think the patio's a good idea."

"I don't really care what you think. I can't stand it in here another minute." On her way through the door, she punched the release bar a little too hard, causing her injured wrist to sting. It was just enough to make her eyes water. Or make her realize they were watering. And once they started there'd be no stopping the tears.

"Hold on," Pete said, coming after her. "If someone followed us, they could be waiting for you to show yourself."

"You're right again, Sheriff." She let her hands slap her thighs, frustrated she couldn't do anything right. More frustrated that he was about to witness a meltdown. She rubbed the protective bandage, determined he'd interpret that as the reason for the tears.

"Come on, Andrea. This isn't my fault."

She knew that and was about to blab it to him. The words weren't going to stop and she wouldn't be able to pick and choose which she said out loud.

"Dang it, I'm not blaming you for anything. I've lost the only job I've ever wanted because I was…I was bored on a Friday night. It's all my fault. I know that." She swiped at the silent tears. Tears for Sharon and a deputy she'd never met. For an injured man who walked out of the desert and died anyway when she wrecked the car. And selfish tears for her lost career. Crying for herself seemed petty, but she couldn't stop.

Before she knew it, Pete had his arms around

her, turning her face into his shoulder. His name tag poked her cheek, but she didn't care. She could smell the starch used on his shirt. Feel the rock-hard muscles again under her palms. It was so easy to be safe wrapped in his arms. It defied logic, but there was nothing logical in anything that had happened since yesterday evening.

Nothing logical at all.

"You can't blame yourself, either, Andrea. If you hadn't volunteered to take Sharon's place, they would have found another way to get to you. It could have been here, surrounded by tourists with lots of kids running everywhere."

Since the fire he'd been professional to the extreme. She preferred him closer with his words a warm whisper against her ear. His hands a steadying force cupping her shoulders. Standing in the circle of his arms seemed both natural and enchanting in spite of the circumstances.

"I wish I'd met you two weeks ago," she said softly into his uniform.

"You might not have found this place so boring." He gently moved her away from hiding her face in his shoulder.

Her chin momentarily rested in the crook of his index finger before he quickly extended his others to circle the back of her neck. Angling her lips closer to his, sweeping down to make a claim.

His lips captured hers, or hers captured his. She didn't care. They meshed together while their bodies screamed to get closer. He was right yet again. If she'd met him when she first arrived in West Texas, she definitely wouldn't have been bored.

"I don't know how many rules we're breaking. At the moment, I'm not really sure I want to know." There was nothing soft about Pete's kiss.

No auditioning necessary.

He was an easy person to like, to admire. Maybe it was a good thing she wasn't sticking around, because she could fall for him. Easy.

The sounds of a helicopter bounced through the mountains. Her father would be here any minute. The Commander hadn't revealed what location she'd be whisked off to. If she was the only person this situation affected, she'd be kicking everyone controlling her life to the curb.

Including the handsome young sheriff holding her in his arms.

"I don't want to go, Pete. I'm not saying that because of the Commander or my dissertation. I haven't wanted to stay with anyone in a long time." She searched his eyes and melted a little more when his dimples appeared. "Have you?"

"I thought that was a pretty good second audition, if I do say so myself." He caught her lips to his again but quickly released them, too. "Just makes me want you on that chopper that much more. You aren't safe here."

"At least give me your number. Do you have a card or something?"

He laughed and shook his head. "You know how to reach me, Andrea."

"True, but Honey doesn't like me. She might not give you the message." She had to joke. They were talking about a call that would never happen. She'd never be allowed to come back to Fort Davis or see the Marfa lights. No matter what position her father held, he'd put her under house arrest before she got close to the border alone.

"Your ride's here." He casually dipped that chiseled chin toward the chest she'd just cried her heart out against. His Adam's apple dipped as he swallowed hard. The brim of his hat cast a shadow over his tanned cheek.

Before he could release her, she leaned in for one last kiss. Pete didn't disappoint. Their lips connected and there wasn't a thought of what they should or shouldn't be doing. Just feeling.

The sad goodbye got her hotter than the desert sun. Then the chopper approached and she recognized the sound. She'd heard it the night before. She'd been racking her brains trying to match the distinct *whomp, whomp, whomp* that had been chasing her. Mixed as it was with the engine noise of Sharon's car, she hadn't been able to distinguish its distinctiveness.

But she knew helicopters and planes. She might not have had much in common with her father... but she had that. It had been their game. They knew their engines.

"That's not my father." Andrea pointed in the direction the chopper was approaching. "You have to trust me, Pete. That's a Hiller, a training helicopter. My dad wouldn't be traveling in anything that small. It only holds three people."

"You know what kind of helicopter just by the sound?"

"What do these idiots want? I can't believe they're coming here in broad daylight with my father ten minutes behind them. It's insane. Do they think they're going to swoop in and—"

Cut off by a shotgun blast, Pete pushed her between him and the building. People eating snacks at the table ran, ducking for cover behind the low brick wall separating them from the field.

"Pete! They don't care who they hurt!"

The doors were a couple of steps away. Another shot burst the brick just above their heads. She ducked to the side, but Pete kept his head down and drew his weapon, retreating to the people pinned down outside.

The gunfire shifted to the other side of the building. Pete searched the direction of the field, stood and helped a family inside the building.

"Everyone back from the windows! Go!" He waved people away from the doors made of glass toward an open classroom. "Get those kids into the classrooms. Everybody stay low. You'll be safe."

"What's going on?" an older man yelled from behind the information desk. "Who's attacking?"

"I'm Sheriff Morrison, Presidio County. Get on the speaker and tell everyone to get to an inside room. Stay away from the windows. No one goes outside. Anyone outside needs to stay in their vehicles."

Pete had her backed up against a wall, literally. He directed people, having holstered his weapon when the threat didn't follow him indoors. He pressed her against the paneling well away from the outer doors.

"I can help. I'm a pretty good shot," she offered.

"You don't leave my sight. That's what they want. Chaos and for me to lose focus. You're the prize, Andrea. They want you for leverage and are obviously willing to risk an open attack."

"I can call the Commander."

"They're listening to the police frequency, maybe even my phone. It's the only way they could have known you were here or that your father was sending a chopper for you."

His body completely blocked her view. She shifted to her right and so did he. Hand on his weapon, ready to go.

"How did they even know who my father is? Oh, God, my ID. They have my name and found out who I am." It really was all her fault. A stupid series of mistakes or events that were ending with innocent people's deaths. "If they are listening, the sooner my father says he's coming, the faster they'll leave. Please, Pete. I can't let anyone else get hurt."

"Here." He shoved his cell between their bodies. "Make it quick. The men after you are aggressive bas—" He cut himself off while two women herded kids into the classroom, shutting the door behind them.

She punched in her father's cell number. "No luck. There's no reception here." She tried to wriggle free from behind Pete's back. "I need the observatory phone."

"Stay where you are, Andrea. Wait, you should get into the classroom with everyone else. You'll be safer and can make the call from there. It sounds like they're landing." Pete moved along the perimeter of the room, closer to the glass patio exit.

She felt exposed, even though she was safe from any gunfire.

"Where are you going?"

"I can't let them enter the building."

She ran across the room to the information desk. "Where are the keys to the doors?"

"Right here," the volunteer answered, slapping the keys on a pile of Star Party pamphlets. "But I ain't getting paid to risk my life."

"Of course not," she said, soothing his hand and looking at his name tag. "But, Ben, can you dial 911? Tell them to find Commander Tony Allen to let him know what's happening. I swear he'll help us."

"Don't even think about locking those front doors, Andrea. That's what they want," Pete instructed, handgun finally drawn and in a ready position. She recognized the stance as the same one her father had taught her. Her gun was inside her travel bag and the bag was on the patio.

"Hurry," she whispered to Ben, who had the landline in his hand but hesitated to reach for the base to dial. "Please."

"It's too dangerous."

"I can do this, Pete. Are they on the ground yet?" She'd feel better if she could get to her gun on the patio.

"What the hell do you think you're doing?" Pete said beside her, taking the keys from her hands. He stood and pulled her back behind the information desk.

"Trying to slow them down."

"Locking the doors won't do that, hon. We don't know what's out there. And I won't let you—or anyone—risk being exposed." He jerked his head at the volunteer still holding the phone. "Get into the classroom and bar the door with anything you can find."

"Yes, sir." Ben crawled extremely fast for an older gentleman.

"Hello?" a voice coming from the receiver yelled. Pete clicked a speaker button. "Morrison here. Did you get through to Commander Allen?"

"They're still trying to locate him. Sheriff and deputies are about twenty minutes out."

"That's what I figured." Pete raised himself far enough to see over the counter. "He's probably with my dad. Try his cell. Tell them we're pinned inside the Observatory Visitor Center. I'm leaving the line open."

Andrea tried to peek over the counter with him, and he shoved her shoulder down before she could get a look. There was nothing to see anyway. Chairs had been knocked over, but the center was empty. This was the first time she actually wished her dad was closer.

PETE SEARCHED THE WALL. Maintenance. Office. Auditorium. Café. He needed someplace safe to hide Andrea before an unknown force burst through the unlocked doors and overpowered them. He wasn't wearing his vest. His dad would tan his hide…if he had one left to hang out to dry.

The extra protectiveness and responsibility weighed on him. It had nothing to do with giving anyone his word. Had nothing to do with his job responsibility. He flat out liked this woman. Everything about her shouted that she was special.

He'd never forgive himself if she was shot or—worse—abducted.

"We've got to get you out of here."

"I am not helpless, Pete. I've been in self-defense courses my entire life. And I know how to shoot. My gun's in the bag we left outside."

Good to know, but he wasn't letting her near that bag. He dropped the key ring on the floor near her hands. "Find one that looks like it's to a regular inside door. Like a broom closet. I'm going to lock you inside."

"Are you sure they're still out there?"

"The chopper's on the ground. The blades are still rotating. No telling how many were already here ready to ambush us." He watched two shadows cross the patio. "Let's move. Next to the snack bar, there's a maintenance door. Run. I'll lay down cover if we need it."

They ran. He could see the shadows but no one followed. Hopefully they didn't have eyes on him or Andrea. He heard the keys and a couple of curses behind him, then a door swung open enough for his charge to squeeze through.

He saw the glint of sun off a mirror outside. They were watching.

"Can you lock the door? Will it lock without the key?"

"I think so."

"Keep the keys with you. I don't need them. Less risky." Bullets could work as a key to unlock, but they might not risk injuring Andrea. He was counting on that.

"But, Pete—"

"Let me do my job, Andrea. Once you're inside, see if you can get into the crawl space. They just saw you open the door. Hide till the cavalry arrives."

"You mean the Navy. He won't let us down," she said from the other side of the door. "This is his thing, after all."

Pete had done all he could do to hide her. Now he needed to protect her. He turned the café tables on their sides. If he had to run, it would give him some cover. The thickest defense was the café counter itself. He plunged over the bar—taking the condiments with him—just as the first shots pierced the windows.

He heard the shouts—in Spanish—and the entrance doors open. More shots, from a machine pistol. The cartel's weapon of choice. Another burst of fire hit the café's menu.

"We know the *chica* is in here. You give her to us and nobody gets hurt."

Pete answered in not so flattering Spanish and blindly fired two rounds toward the front. He was answered with another burst from a machine pistol and plenty of curses.

Static over his radio. Maybe the cavalry would arrive sooner than he'd anticipated. He couldn't make out any words, but he turned the volume down so none of his adversaries would hear them when he could. He spoke into the microphone with a low voice. "This is Morrison. Pinned in the café. Numerous civilians in the classroom area. No eyes on multiple hostiles with machine pistols."

"We know it's you and you be all alone, Sheriff. We got no problem with you, man. We just want the girl."

"Didn't hear me the first time?" He popped off two rounds over the counter again, preserving his ammo. Cursing exploded from his opponents, followed by scrambling. "Why her?"

"No help's getting up the mountain."

So did they know about Commander Allen's helicopter or not? He knew how many rounds he had left. There wasn't much he could do until they made a move on the door.

Rapid fire pinned him to the floor, ricocheting off metal objects in the kitchen. His biggest worry yesterday had been if he'd have a job after the election. Today the only future he was worried about was surviving the next couple of hours.

And making certain Andrea did, too.

Chapter Eleven

Andrea could hear them through the door. Balancing on the mop bucket wasn't easy, but it did get her close enough to the ceiling to push the tile to the side. Her wrist ached before the men trying to kill her had landed. She was extremely aware of every tendon as she did a chin-up into the ceiling.

Her muscles shook with the strain. She bit her lip to silence the grunt of pain. She spread her weight over the steel supports, breathing hard, wanting nothing more than to roll over to her back and rest. But that wasn't an option.

Silently, she moved the tile back into place. Shouting. More gunfire sounding like a machine gun. *Come on, Commander! Where are you?*

The ceiling wasn't the safest place. One wrong move and she could fall through. One wrong sound would alert the men with the automatic weapons that could penetrate the tiles hiding her.

So she needed a way out.

They both did. That rapid fire would cut through

Pete in a matter of seconds. She heard him, heard his weapon. He was still alive, but for how long? She could do this. She wasn't your average astronomy PhD student. She'd never been average, with a dad who trained her well. She could shoot and hold her own in a fight. If those men were on the inside of the center, then she needed to get to the outside and her gun.

"PETE, PETE, ARE you there? We're in the parking lot. You doing okay, son?" His dad's voice was a welcome reprieve from the bullets flying over his head.

"Just great."

"Let's assume they're tuned in to our frequency, son. Let's change it up. Remember the colt's birthday last month?"

"Do it."

Pete changed frequencies on the hand radio. They wouldn't have long before the men sitting on top of him would circle through the numbers and overhear.

"Pete? You know what these guys want?"

"Yeah, Andrea. Is Commander Allen with you?"

"Separate entry point. How many?"

"Four that arrived by chopper. I don't know about outside."

"We've cleared the parking lot and are ready to evacuate the classroom through the emergency exit. Change frequency to Peach's birthday."

"Got it." Pete twisted the dial again. It was another date easily remembered. They had just celebrated it last week.

"Sit tight, Pete. Just sit tight. We'll have you out of there in two shakes."

He checked his rounds. Three remained.

He'd left his extra clips in the truck and hadn't been prepared for a shoot-out.

Sit tight. As if he had a choice. He heard low grumbling in Spanish, words he couldn't distinguish other than complaints about a madwoman. Shuffling.

"Who's out there?" one of the men asked in English.

Pete slid to the edge of the counter and peered around, expecting one of the Jeff Davis deputies to be in a position to take these guys down. Shocker of shocks. Andrea drew her hand out of her bag and raised a weapon.

Three shots. That was all he had to get to her. He couldn't stay put. She fired, and he ran straight through the shattered door under her cover. She stood at the ready, waiting for him.

A fifth man came around the brick wall, a large gun barrel pointed at them. "Down!" Pete shouted. He reached Andrea, they spun, the man fired, Andrea fired.

The bullet seared Pete's flesh and knocked him sideways. Their assailant fell to the patio concrete. Pete managed to stay on his feet and kept them moving forward. "Run!"

They both took cover at the wall of the ramp leading to the closest telescopes. A five-foot-wide path bordered on either side with a three-foot-high brick wall that was one foot thick. It would stop a spray of machine-pistol bullets.

Too much space. Wide-open fields. No cover.

But if he jumped the brick wall he could draw fire and possibly disable their helicopter. Andrea could make it to the front of the building and his father.

"Follow the sidewalk to the front. Deputies are on sight evacuating the civilians."

One of the men jumped through the glass, and Pete tugged Andrea to the ground behind the brick. He covered her with his body. They heard several rounds and saw red shards splinter into the air. The strength in his left arm where he'd been shot was waning.

"Where are you going?" Andrea didn't seem fazed. She spoke from under the protection of his body, taking everything that happened with a deep breath and calm logic.

"We need a distraction so you can get around front," he answered, breathing hard from the exertion. "I'm heading to their ride and you're heading to my dad."

"The helicopter? Can you fly that old relic? I can."

He shook his head. "But I can disable it. We go on three."

"But I said I could fly—"

When a new blast broke more of the brick into splinters, he ducked his head again, reaching around Andrea, tugging her closer, covering as much of her body as he could. If she wouldn't cooperate, he'd take her to the front himself. The men might be able to escape, but that wasn't his highest priority. Getting Andrea to safety was.

The burst ended and he moved past her, clasping her hand with his right to get her started in a low crouch below the wall and up the path. His left arm was getting harder to move, but he still had clear vision and a clear head. "I don't need your help. We need to move."

She tugged him to a stop. "You're getting my help, so don't argue. I don't want those men to get away. So, do you want to jump the wall or go around the far end by the telescopes? I'm thinking jumping is faster. I'll lay down a cover while you run."

"Hand me your gun." He stuck his weapon in its holster and covered her weapon with his hand. "I'll disable the chopper. You're going around front."

She placed the handle of her Glock in his. "We're wasting time. It's not a one-way ticket if I fly that hunk of junk out of here. Cover me."

Spunk or confidence or just plain stubbornness. He didn't know which. She stuck her head up, evidently didn't see anyone and took off, crossing the path and rolling over the brick wall separating it from the field. He didn't have the chance to stop her and didn't think he could have. He hadn't radioed his dad to say they'd left the building.

He stood a little slower than normal—probably the blood loss—he could see it soaking through the sleeve of his shirt. He backed to the opposite wall, keeping his eyes on the doorway to the Visitor Center. He heard gunfire, but from the opposite side of the building.

Those men would want to make their escape... fast. They'd be heading toward their escape, and Andrea was almost at the chopper. Dammit, all they had to do was sit tight as his dad had instructed.

A man came through the door again. Pete fired two shots, breaking the glass next to him. His aim was off, missing the man's body mass, but he'd forced him back inside. Maybe he was closer to passing out than he'd thought. The chopper was warming up. Pete ran, firing his last rounds that kept the machine pistol inside the building silent.

Now, if he could just keep his feet moving.

FORTUNATELY, THE HILLER wasn't that far and there wasn't anyone inside it to deal with. The man who had come up behind her had probably been left to stand guard. Andrea concentrated on getting ready to get in the air and let Pete deal with the men wanting to kill her.

Pete opened the opposite door and slowly climbed inside. "You sure you can fly this thing?"

He leaned on the door, so tired his head thudded against the plastic.

"Definitely. Buckle up." She didn't wait on him, moving the stick and lifting into the air.

They were away from the observatory in seconds. She could hear machine gun fire but didn't hover to see how many men or find out what they looked like. The former sheriff could round up the bad guys.

She was a bit rusty, but it felt good to be behind a stick again. She'd loved flying with her dad while she was growing up. He'd take her into the air with him as often as he could get private fly time. He'd been Dad then, back before he'd permanently become the Commander.

"Hey, I meant it when I said buckle up, Pete." She swatted his arm to get his attention. Her hand came back bloody. "You were shot? Stay with me, Sheriff! Don't you dare pass out."

He didn't answer. She took a quick glance at her passenger, who was seriously slumped toward his door. Shoot, she wasn't even certain he'd closed the thing correctly. He was out cold.

There were a couple of wild bumps as she jerked him closer to the middle. It was a nervous couple of minutes as she looped his arm through the seat's shoulder strap.

One thing missing on the Hiller was the radio. She couldn't call anyone. She couldn't reach Pete's cell phone and couldn't see his department radio.

"I guess I should put this thing down somewhere and try to keep you alive."

The controls weren't responding as fast as she would have liked. They were as sluggish as peddling through pudding. They had probably been hit by the last gunfire as they were taking off. She wouldn't let them crash. But wherever she set this thing down, they were going to be trapped there.

Stuck without medical supplies, food or water. Each minute they were in the air, the controls got worse.

"Hold on, Pete. We're going to land."

Chapter Twelve

Soft lips. Pete wasn't too familiar with being awakened by a kiss, but he recognized the sweetness. He reached out with his arms to catch Andrea's body and hissed between his teeth instead. The pain in his left arm was manageable, but he'd rather not push it.

"I was shot."

"Yes, you were. I've been patiently waiting for you to wake up. But let me tell you, it was getting pretty boring around here again without your company."

"Can't have that." He sat up with a little help from Andrea. "We know what happens when you get bored."

"Ha. Ha. Ha," she said, plopping down next to him and crossing her legs.

He carefully lifted his arm without the same pain he'd experienced a few minutes earlier. The chopper was thirty or forty yards away, seemingly intact. Drag marks from his boots left a trail to where they currently sat. He'd be lucky if there weren't holes in his jeans.

"I'm sort of glad I wasn't awake for that." He nodded toward the chopper.

"We've been here awhile. I couldn't leave you baking in the sun. You lost your hat."

"It's late afternoon already." They had an hour, maybe an hour and a half of light left before the sun was obscured by the mountains.

"That's right, tough guy." She swayed into his good arm before bringing her knees up and resting on them. "You finally got that nap you needed."

"No cell reception?"

"No nothing reception." She pointed to the department radio, then jumped up to retrieve it. "I thought for sure the Commander would be swooping in for the ultimate I-told-you-so. But I haven't heard anything except a cow mooing."

"Thanks for fixing my arm."

"I can't believe you were shot. Okay, never mind, I can believe it. I mean, there were a lot of bullets flying around. You should have told me when it happened. You might have at least tried to tell me before I ran to the Hiller. Though, honestly, I don't think I gave you time to tell me—"

"Andrea," he said, covering her hand with his good one. She was talking fast without taking a breath. Nervous or scared or maybe a little of both.

"Yeah?"

"You didn't shoot me. We got out of there and I doubt those men escaped. There was nowhere for them to run when you took the helicopter.

"Can I assume something's wrong with that thing?" He pointed toward the chopper.

"One of those men shot the engine before we got safely away. Well, almost safely away. We were very lucky, considering he could have sliced that trainer in half with his machine gun."

"Machine pistol. We've known they were smuggling those for some time, but it was the first time I'd faced one."

"How's your arm? You know, you were lucky. The bullet tore a hunk of your flesh away. You'll just have a wicked scar." She picked up a pebble and tossed it across the path. "But I got the bleeding stopped and didn't have to dig around with a penknife for a bullet. And believe me, I could have, too. My dad saw fit that I have lots of practical survival training."

"I see that. You're pretty good with a gun, too." He held her hand, resting it on his thigh. "Come on, just catch your breath and give me a minute to figure this out."

"Oh, sorry. I'm babbling again, aren't I? I do better when I'm moving. Less stressed." She tried to release his fingers with the intent of getting to her feet. "I'm not certain why you passed out. It bled a lot, but did you hit your head or something?"

"I'm fine. Don't worry about it." Pete kept a firm grip on her hand, wanting her next to him for multiple reasons, but touching her skin was the first one that came to mind. "Give me a second. Then we'll take a look around. See if I recognize where we are." He knew they hadn't flown far and were still pretty much close to nowhere.

"Oh, I know exactly where we're at," she said with confidence.

He knew the peaks, the general vicinity. "Maybe twenty-five miles northeast from the observatory."

"Very good, Sheriff."

"I've traveled these mountains enough to recognize the terrain. That puts us darn close to the Scout ranch. We'll need to get started up one of those trails if we want to sleep in a bed tonight."

"Is that an invitation?" She winked. "If so, I think you could at least buy a girl dinner first."

"I've already bought you breakfast," he teased in return. "But I'm sure your father will have strong words objecting to your spending another night in Marfa."

He groaned as he stood up. Feeling like he hadn't slept in a week and that he was as old as sin. Andrea helped him until he was steady on his feet.

"You know, I am an adult. I make decisions all on my own."

"Maybe we should start with dinner after we determine exactly why those men would make such a stupid move today."

"I can go with that."

"No radio in the helicopter?" he asked as they passed it. She answered with a look and a long sigh. "Right. First thing you would have tried."

They headed up the trail. He was a lot weaker than he could let on, but they needed higher ground for cell reception.

"You okay?"

"I'll manage." He would.

"Mind if I stay close to make sure you do?" She shouldered up next to his right side.

"Going to hold my hand?"

"Maybe." She smiled.

"Why hasn't your father found you yet?"

"I've been asking myself the same question."

"I'll take your Glock back." He extended his palm.

She slapped her hand on his, wrapping her fingers tight and keeping hold. "No offense, Pete, but I think I'll keep it. You aren't quite yourself at the moment."

Perhaps she was right. She was definitely right about him not being one hundred percent. He'd seen her shoot. They'd both hit their target on the café patio and she hadn't fallen to pieces when the body hit the ground. He didn't know yet how he actually felt about shooting someone. It wasn't like they'd had much time to think about their actions. Their assailant had been attempting to kill them. They didn't need to think about it at the moment, either. There'd be plenty of time later.

"So, I've been thinking, since I haven't had much else to do all afternoon waiting on you to wake up."

Unless he wanted to walk home, they had another

good fifteen-minute hike before they got a phone signal. They'd never manage a call at the bottom of one of these gullies, even if it was the easiest route home.

"What conclusion did you come to?" He was gaining confidence with each step. Up it was and then down the other side to the Scout camp he'd gone to in his youth.

She took a step away from him, angling toward a path cows and horses had beaten over time. "You can't be serious?"

He pointed toward the butte. "E.T. should phone home."

She faced him with both hands on her hips. "You are never going to let me live down that *aliens* were chasing me, are you?"

He laughed. Really laughed. There was something about the way she stood there along with the way she held her mouth and tilted her head. "No, I don't think I am."

She didn't ask if he was up to the climb, just took a step and looped her bandaged wrist through his right arm. One wobbly step at a time, he stayed on his feet.

"As I was saying, I've had a lot of time to think. When the *aliens* showed up at the observatory—" she used her original description of the men trying to kill her without skipping a beat "—it didn't make a lot of sense."

"How did they know you were leaving? And why

are they trying to grab you?" They kept a steady pace on the inclined path. "After we make the call, we need to take cover. We can't be certain they aren't listening to my phone, but it's more likely they were monitoring the police bands."

"Right. So we're thinking along the same lines."

"You're a valuable asset just because of your father. But why risk losing men and a helicopter?"

"Exactly. They might think I know something, yet killing me would be the fastest, most reliable way to eliminate that threat."

He'd never met anyone like her. She wasn't upset or falling apart. "Does this happen to you all the time?"

"Hardly. I grew up preparing for it, though. I wanted to please my parents and did everything possible to make them proud."

"Like learning to fly helicopters?"

"That's actually fun. All of it has been to some degree, I guess." She squeezed his biceps. "You'll have to tell me about your treks into the mountains sometime. Right now, concentrate on breathing. We'll have time to get to know each other later."

He was surprised how much he wanted that to be true. "The aliens either think you know something or they wanted to hold you hostage in order to exchange you for something."

"That is the same conclusion I came to earlier. Unfortunately, neither of those reasons explains why they attacked in broad daylight using a helicopter.

I mean, wouldn't it have made more sense to enter through the door, take us by surprise and then signal for the chopper once they were successful?"

He stopped and checked his pockets for the phone.

"Looking for this?" She handed him his cell after pulling it from her back pocket. "I turned it off to save the battery."

He turned it on, then continued their climb. He wanted this point to be high enough for a connection but it wasn't. They climbed in silence for a while, thinking. "You're right. Their attack doesn't make sense. They would have assured themselves of your location, been ready to get in and out, not hang back. They could have overrun me easily."

"Unless it's all a diversion."

"You're brilliant." She was gorgeous and brilliant. The phone was ready. He pulled up his dad's cell number and tapped the speaker.

"Pete?"

"Hey, Dad."

"Thank God. Is Andrea with you?"

"We're both great. I think my cell might be compromised."

"We assumed communications weren't safe. Do you know your location?"

"Yeah, I could go for a Buffalo swim if it were open."

"Ah, gotcha. Nicely done, son. We'll be there ASAP." Andrea looked around, obviously wondering about his coded message.

"Sort of wondered why you haven't found us already," he asked his dad.

"We lost the helicopter soon after takeoff. Took us until about half an hour ago to discover that neither of you was with the last man who escaped to the south."

"Five men. Three in the chopper and two in a vehicle?"

"Correct and all accounted for. Commander Allen wants to talk to his daughter."

"Are you all right, Andrea?" her father asked.

"Yes, sir. Not a scratch."

"That's my girl. Mechanical difficulties?"

"Yes, sir."

"The search team got a late start. We'll steer them to you soon. You're certain you're fine?"

"She's brilliant, sir," Pete answered when he noticed the tears in Andrea's eyes. "We better save the battery, sir. Just in case."

"Certainly." He disconnected.

"HE'S NOT MUCH for goodbyes." Andrea used a knuckle to wipe the moisture from her eyes. Pete might get the wrong impression...or the right one. Either way, she could break down later. Think about everything...later.

With the exception that Pete thought she was brilliant.

"This is a pretty good place to wait. If you hear the wrong helicopter again, we can dart down this side of the hill." He nodded behind her. "Closer to the road."

She squinted, noticing the buildings at the bottom of the canyon. There was a well-marked trail zigzagging down. "You mean I was one hill away from civilization?"

"Yeah, but to its credit, it was a large hill." He was still breathing hard from their hike, but smiling.

"We're resting. Sit." They chose one of the smoother rocks and kept their backs to the sun. It was quiet. A gentle wind was the only sound. If whoever was chasing her did understand Pete's description of their location, she'd be able to hear them straightaway.

"So, a diversion? That makes sense."

"Whatever happened this afternoon had to be a profitable enough deal to sacrifice five men and a helicopter. It wasn't rigged for the light show they used to imitate the phenomenon near Marfa. It sounded like this type of Hiller, but this one is bare bones."

"So they have another chopper."

"It's logical to assume so."

"Whoever's behind this discovered who you were and used the opportunity presented to them to their advantage." Pete wiped his brow. "Are you certain you don't have experience being a detective?"

"I had an hour and a half to myself, and deductive reasoning just happens to be my strength."

"So your switching places with Sharon last night

was purely coincidental. If I were them, I might assume you work at the observatory. I don't think I'd assume you're the daughter of a director with Homeland Security."

"Sharon. Sharon knew. I talked about it last week. About how difficult it was for me to convince the university to let me come, since my dad was opposed." She had to move, so she jumped to her feet. "Shoot. I forgot the first rule my dad taught me. IIc's been paranoid about my mother and me since he joined the DHS. Afraid someone would attempt exactly what they did today."

"Then we can't assume Sharon's switching with you was a coincidence. This might have been the plan all along."

"They couldn't have known I'd say yes. And what about the man in the desert?" She walked a few feet and tugged a long leaf off a bush, nervously tearing the ends off.

"He's an undercover agent who discovers the plan to abduct his commander's daughter. I can think of a lot of reasons he'd risk warning someone. So last night the aliens aren't smuggling drugs across the border, they're searching for an escaped hostage—your dad's undercover man. He's got details they can't let be exposed, but he finds his way to you. They run you off the road and would have abducted you."

"But you came along. They don't know that the

agent didn't tell me anything, but they want to make certain."

"Somehow they know he's Homeland Security and send someone in posing as..."

"The phony agent," they said together.

"How would they have known he was DHS? Your dad's man from the desert was pretty beat up. They could have gotten the info from him." Pete stood, shaded his eyes and checked out the terrain behind him. "Then again, it makes more sense that they discovered him if he was trying to warn your dad about the danger you were in."

"If all of this is just coincidence, though... Why is Sharon still missing?"

Not answering said more than trying to soothe her guilty conscience. He thought Sharon was dead. Once they got the necessary information from her, they wouldn't need her any longer. "Do you think they killed Sharon or that she was working with them?"

"I don't believe these men think twice about eliminating anyone who stands in their way."

"I'm sorry one of those people was your deputy. Logan seemed nice."

"I had to cover for him a lot. Now I know why. He was a good kid. I didn't have much else to do. If I hadn't worked all night, I'd be up taking care of ranch chores. I'd rather ride on patrol."

He lifted an eyebrow, smiled and she knew the

subject was changing. "Hey, you going to share how you got outside from the maintenance closet?"

She waved her injured wrist. "Let me tell you, it wasn't easy. Good thing I can pull my own weight, injured or not. Once I got into the crawl space and found a way to the roof, I climbed down the steel beams that formed the partial shade over the door. They were at a slant and got me close enough to the ground that I could drop."

"Is that the Commander's chopper?" he asked, facing the south to catch a glimpse. She nodded, and he dusted off his jeans with his good hand. "You're a very competent, capable woman."

"Tell that to my father." She followed him back the way they'd come. There was plenty of room for another chopper to land. "He's going to command me to leave. I doubt he'll hang around long enough to drop you by the hospital."

"I don't blame him."

"I'm not certain I'm leaving." There was too much unfinished business here. "I don't want to run away."

"Of course you should." He stopped, grabbing her upper arms, wincing at the sudden movement of his own injury. "Seven men are dead. You can't just shrug that off. It's dangerous for you here."

"Whatever reason they had to abduct me, it's gone now."

"You don't know that." His grip tightened, but it didn't hurt. It seemed he was fighting to keep her at arm's length. She would have preferred to be pulled next to his chest.

"But you agreed with me."

The chopper was getting closer.

"A good guess doesn't mean we're correct." His good hand cupped her shoulder.

"I know you're right." Then why was the first thought in her head how to ditch her new escort that hadn't even been assigned to her yet? Then find a way back to Pete's place. She didn't even know where Pete's place was. "What if I don't go back with my father?"

"But you agreed—" Pete searched her eyes and she wasn't certain what he saw, but he dropped his hands to his sides. "Come on, Andrea. What would be gained from staying? You have nothing to prove."

She didn't want to stay just for Pete. She barely knew him. But her heart dropped when he started back down the path, leaving her to follow again. "How are you going to catch the men responsible for Logan's death? What about Sharon? You said I was good at this detective stuff."

"Do you really think your father's going to allow you to stay? He was packing you off before the attack. There's no way he's saying yes."

That was true. She'd rarely stood up to her parents. Their advice was usually firm and logical. So there had never been a reason to question them. The exception was when her father had declared she couldn't come to West Texas in person. Perhaps if he'd explained his reasons instead of dictating, seven men wouldn't be dead and a young woman wouldn't still be missing.

"There's one thing that everyone around me keeps forgetting. You can't force me to leave the observatory."

Chapter Thirteen

There had been many times throughout Pete's teen-age years that he'd argued with his dad. During the past six weeks, he'd been holding back because of his dad's heart attack, but he was building up to a doozy of a fight. If he confronted him, he'd been thinking that all hell would break loose.

"They still at it?" Honey asked from her desk.

"I didn't know people could yell that long without a drink or shot of tequila," his dad joked.

Andrea and her father might not have the exact family problems, but they definitely had a lot of words to *share*. If he'd known, he would have taken them to the middle of the desert for this confrontation instead of his dad's old office.

The door flew open and the Commander marched out, eyes front without any acknowledgment as he passed them. Pete had no illusions. That was not the expression of a man who had achieved his goal—which was to get Andrea on the next transport home.

Commander Allen executed a one-eighty to be face-to-face with him. "You should get that wound seen to." His voice was void of inflection yet full of buried emotion.

Or maybe it was just Pete's own anxiety pushing its way onto others. He didn't need the responsibility of an attractive woman in his life or workplace. It was time for decisions.

"She's determined to stay," Allen continued. "And mad as hell at me because she's not."

"Yes, sir. I understand your frustration." She wasn't going to be his responsibility. That was good. Very good. His personal desire didn't amount to anything in this decision.

"I need coffee before round two."

"Does it matter if it's good?" his dad asked.

"I'm used to the worst."

"Around the corner and you'll smell the sludge," his dad directed but walked beside the Commander, who threw back his head laughing at something else his father had said.

Pete could only scratch his head.

"Everyone show up for their shift?" he asked Honey. "When will the Griggs family arrive?" Could he pull off business as usual? Swing by the café for a break without the rest of the town asking what the hell was going on? He needed a minute to take care of his responsibilities. Another minute to think. But where? His best bet for a reprieve was his house.

"Yes, and in about forty-five minutes," Honey answered.

No time to make it to the house and back. He needed a real meal, not just a package of pretzels from the vending machine, before he could face Logan's parents. He glanced up to see Andrea standing in the office doorway and then their dads rounded the corner with smiles on both their faces.

"Pete, would you join me a minute?" Andrea's father asked, gesturing to the office.

Did anyone lower on the totem pole ever tell this man no?

"We've been tracking a high number of gun purchases by a few individuals. We believe something big's in the works, that the cartel is tired of receiving their guns one or two at a time. Homeland likes your distraction theory, Pete," Commander Allen stated once the door was closed.

Pete kept his hands tucked in his armpits and his mouth shut. Andrea had let her father believe he had thought up the distraction angle. He was sure they both sort of followed that trail together.

"We checked out some satellite pictures and discovered a large number of trucks crossing the border at Presidio into Manuel Ojinaga. You were right. They wanted us focused on the attempted abduction instead of the payment delivery for a major drug deal. I think it's time I brought you onto the team, Sheriff."

There wasn't any doubt which sheriff their visitor from Homeland Security was directing his comment to. Pete caught himself swallowing hard, nervous. He knew his job and his county and didn't have anything to feel nervous about. Nothing except losing everything if DHS checked into his background.

Pete understood the sideways glance from his father. A look that said keep your mouth shut and let me do the talking.

Easy for his dad, who had kept his mouth shut for over twenty-six years. He'd kept a secret that could potentially destroy them both. Andrea sat in his father's chair, head down, not making eye contact.

"I'm setting up a task force and I need you to be a part of it."

Pete snapped his attention back to the Commander. "You need me. Why?"

"You're familiar with the area and think on your feet. We need some of that and someone to coordinate with the other county sheriffs or local police."

"Thank you, sir, but I have to pass. My plate's about as full as it can get right now." He ignored his dad's attempt to get his attention. "I have work to do. I'm actually in charge of a few things around here and need to get ready for Logan's family. Excuse me."

The two older men parted, and he passed between them.

"Maybe I should explain?" Andrea asked behind him.

"No, this one's my responsibility," his dad said. "Wait here a minute, will ya?" He followed him out the door. "Son, this is a great op—"

Pete bit down hard—teeth on teeth. He knew where the conversation was headed and didn't want to have it publicly, so he pushed through to the locker room. His dad caught the employee only door before it slammed in his face. Pete verified no one was there so they could talk freely. "You're really for me joining a Homeland task force?"

"Of course I am. It's a big step for you."

"It's a family power struggle. She wants to stay, he wants her to go. The last thing I need is to be around any of that mess." He lowered his voice. "Especially involved with the daughter of one of the top dogs in Homeland Security."

"She's leaving with her father. Besides, no one's going to uncover who you really are. You don't need to think of that right now."

"Hell, Dad, it's all I ever think about since you dropped this bomb on me."

"Keeping your identity a secret is for your own safety."

He dropped his hands onto his dad's shoulders. The muscle under his fingertips was less solid than two months ago. A lot less solid than two years ago. He shook his head. He wasn't a crying man—neither one of them was. But the only man he'd ever called family stared at him with his brown eyes about to overflow.

"I love you, you old coot. But I already know who I am and who my biological father was. I've just been waiting for you to tell me why it all happened."

"How did you find out?"

"I'm the sheriff. At least that's what you all are telling me. It didn't take much investigating to discover where I came from twenty-six years ago or the identity of the man I assume was my biological father."

"We'll talk about that at a more appropriate time. Right now Commander Allen needs your help." Pride or excitement or envy weaved its way into his father's words. Maybe because of the times their department had been overlooked for opportunities like this one.

Would his dad be let down to know that it was Andrea's idea and had nothing to do with the Commander's need for help?

"What happens if he decides to run a background check on me? What then? How much trouble are you going to be in? You're right. This isn't the place to talk about forging our relationship with the Department of Homeland Security or why that's impossible. The best thing is to bow out and assist where needed."

His dad's face grew older under the fluorescent lights. "I know you have a lot of questions, but you're right. This is a talk more appropriate for home. I do wish you'd reconsider working on the task force."

"Not a chance. It's just a disaster waiting to happen."

"It can't be all bad, son." His dad winked. "I've seen the way his daughter looks at you."

"You haven't seen anything. And it'll never happen. It might have been fun while she was here, but I have no future. A woman like that needs a future." He couldn't risk the complications of becoming involved with the daughter of such a powerful man.

"What are you talking about? You have job security here. You're running unopposed."

"Let's drop it." Now wasn't the time to tell his dad he hadn't submitted the election paperwork to run for sheriff. He hadn't decided—yet—if he would. But he could set him straight on one thing. "I'm not getting involved with anyone, especially Andrea Allen. My babysitting days are long behind me."

Ouch. Andrea was careful not to allow the door to slam, hearing a gentle clicking noise as it closed. She'd completely misread their friendship. Following him to apologize, ready to abide by her father's wishes and leave Marfa, she hadn't meant to eavesdrop, especially on a father-and-son chat that seemed very private. But now she was glad she'd overheard Pete say he wasn't getting involved with anyone…especially her.

Now she was having second or third or fourth thoughts. She'd lost track of how many times she'd changed her mind about staying here. It was as if her decision-making ability had evaporated with one look at Pete's dimples.

Pete's earlier look of disappointment had deflated her desire to be around him. She'd thought staying in the area worked to everyone's advantage. Before the shooting at the observatory, she thought she'd keep her promise to her father and get her dissertation finished and maybe allow a few distractions with the sheriff.

Not anymore. Not now that she knew those men were willing to kill anyone. And not now that she knew how Pete really felt.

It could be all business for her and not matter who stood guard outside the telescope. No. She was acting like a scorned lover. Staying meant putting more people at risk and she couldn't do that. She'd have to find another way to obtain telescope time.

It wouldn't be the end of everything if she finished up the thesis in Austin. But she could be disappointed for not being able to finish here. She couldn't stay. It would be horribly selfish. She hit the employees only door as she pushed it open again, catching Pete with a hand on the other side and a surprised look on his face.

"You aren't going to talk me into joining his task force," Pete said to his father, then turning to Andrea, "and neither are you."

"I came to apologize before leaving Marfa. But now…"

"Nothing to apologize for. Excuse me."

"Man, you really are something." She blocked the door. Pete could have moved her easily but seemed reluctant to.

"Can you leave us alone a minute, Dad?"

The retiring sheriff squeezed past. Pete clasped hands with her, gently pulling her to where the door could shut with a loud bang. She shook his hand free as quickly as she could.

"You don't need to be talked into anything." She knew what calls her father would make as soon as they all left the office. "The people who sign your paychecks are already being contacted. You no longer have a choice."

"Why is this so important to you?"

"Not me. I don't force myself on anyone. My dad's limiting the number of people who know about the incident. You're already a part of his small circle. It's logical—therefore, it'll happen."

"As much as I hate that logic, I understand it."

"Oh, and don't worry about having to be around me. You know you can assign anyone you want as my *babysitter*. It doesn't matter to me." Telling him she'd changed her mind and wouldn't be heading back was on the tip of her tongue. "I really don't understand why you're so reluctant to help the Commander. This is an amazing opportunity that could take you places. After this is over you could name your assignment."

"I'll make sure Commander Allen gets the help he needs. And who says I want to leave Marfa? That's a lot of presuming you're doing after knowing me for such a short time. I actually like it here."

He smiled, and her heart melted a little. He was delightful when he wanted to be, but right now was obviously not one of those times.

"You should use that wicked charm of yours more often, especially with strangers. I bet your father and the rest of the community who raised you gave in every time you smiled. Is that why you're so spoiled?"

"Me? You think *I'm* spoiled?" His deep voice rose a couple of octaves with that accusation. "Where do you get off calling anyone spoiled? Have you taken a look at the way you have your father wrapped around your pinkie finger? Never mind, I don't care to know the answer. It's not worth it."

"Man, do you have that wrong. I don't call him the Commander because of his rank."

Andrea didn't really think Pete was spoiled. She was hurt from his private remarks to his father and she was striking out. She wanted to apologize, take it back, tell him she didn't mean it. But she couldn't. She'd thought he'd liked her and the wound was too fresh.

Later. She'd apologize later. She'd calm down while looking into deep space or on the plane back to Austin. She was still uncertain which route was in her future.

"If you'll excuse me, I need to get in touch with the observatory. I've already confirmed that my telescope will be ready at seven-thirty and need to make arrangements." Arrangements for the information and her things to be sent to her, but she wouldn't admit that to him. She reached for the door. His arm stopped her. She spun to face him, landing against his chest, looking straight at that dimpled chin.

"You aren't going anywhere on your own. You can wait in the office while I make the arrangements."

"Fine."

"Okay."

Earlier today, being this close would have ended in some serious kissing. The disappointment she was experiencing that it was no longer a possibility froze her in place. She focused her stare at his chin, unable to meet his eyes.

His hands were snug around her waist and she was ready to forgive him and explain her harsh words. Ready for those kisses to take over and there not be a need for any explanations from either of them. Then he gently moved her to the side.

If she had looked at him, she might have known that he was trying to open the door. By the time she figured it out, she added embarrassment to the long list of emotions she was scrolling through.

"You stick with me or your dad until I find a deputy to escort you. Or you can wait in a locked office."

Without uttering a word, she veered left, choosing to stand near Reception instead of sitting in the chair waiting on her father to finish his calls. Pete went about his business, giving instructions, signing some papers…man-in-charge stuff. When he was done, the mayor or someone equivalent called to speak to him. He looked at the glass front doors and told Peach—the sisters had switched positions—to take a message.

A couple entered the front. The man's face looked confused and the woman cried into an old-fashioned handkerchief. Peach pointed to Pete without a word. He tapped on the open office door and brought a third chair inside.

"Sorry, Commander Allen, but I need this room for a bit."

Her father glanced at the couple and left, walking to a corner, placing another phone call on his cell while she watched Pete hug each of them before they sat.

"Logan's parents. They wanted to talk to Pete about what happened," Peach said softly next to her.

"I wish I'd known him better."

"He was a nice young man. They're still searching for the student he was on a date with," Peach stated, then answered the phone.

Andrea's guilt was growing. She'd been so caught up in her own world she hadn't thought about Sharon or that her body hadn't been found. Had she been abducted or murdered and her body dumped in a remote spot? They might never know, but she had to find out.

Chapter Fourteen

"Is there another office my father could use, Peach?"

"Sure." She pulled open a drawer and handed Andrea a key. "Through the back hallway next to Pete's office, then second door on the right."

Andrea tugged gently on her father's sleeve, and he followed, arguing with someone else for a change. She sat in a straight-back chair and let him take a seat behind the desk, waiting for him to finish the call.

"I'm staying. I was going to return with you, until I saw Logan's parents. I meant what I said. I think you should come up with a plan and let me help find Sharon or whoever abducted or murdered her. Will you let me do this and include me?"

The office was empty except for the desk and chairs. No pictures of Pete on the wall to distract her.

"Why do you think you're qualified to help?"

"I don't, but those men were after me for some reason today. They might be again."

"Therein lies the problem. You aren't safe here," the Commander stated firmly. His men never argued with that tone, but it always brought out the rebellious teenager in her.

"I don't want you to be disappointed with me again."

"Why do you think I would be?"

"I thought… Well, you and Mom argued so vehemently against my coming out here." She looked at the secrets he hid beneath the stoic naval-commander expression. "Oh my gosh. You couldn't tell me the real reason you didn't want me to come."

"No, I couldn't. I'm not supposed to speak about it now. I had a man undercover and I knew how explosive this region is. I didn't want you in danger."

"I have to do this, Dad."

He reluctantly nodded. "My boss is twisting my arm to get you to cooperate. They want to use you for bait."

"It's not very appealing or noble when you put it like that."

He stood and pulled her to her feet. "Andrea, this is serious. You aren't trained to be an operative, and any number of things can go wrong. Probably will go wrong. We've already lost a very experienced agent."

"I know, Dad. I just don't think I could live with myself if I walked away. Could you?"

He shook his head. She liked it when Commander Allen left the room and he was her father again.

"Whoever's arranging for this gun shipment to Mexico has to be high up in the cartel."

"I wish you'd reconsider." Her father's voice dropped so soft she could barely hear.

"You let me think you were the overprotective commander to try to keep me from coming. You've got to remember that I'm your daughter. I need to do this. The entire time I was growing up I heard you say how important it was to finish what you started, to be a part of a team and not leave anyone behind. How can you ask me to walk away from all three of the most important things to you?" She wanted to hug him, but they really didn't hug a lot in her family.

"The most important thing to me is keeping the two women I love the most safe from harm. What kind of father would deliberately let his daughter be abducted by drug dealers?"

"One who understands how much this means to me. I can make a difference. Please let me help."

He gave a reluctant nod. "For you. Not for the men twisting my arm. I do understand about not leaving a man behind. Responsibility can sometimes weigh you down. I should have a team with you every moment—that's what your mother would want—but we're shorthanded as it is. Would you consider a professional bodyguard...would you allow—I see by your expression that's not a possibility, either."

"You know a military detail or bodyguard won't

allow these men to feel comfortable enough to act. I'll finish the study at the observatory. I promise I won't leave until you're ready for me to draw out these murderers again. I'll call as often as you need me to. I don't want to be a burden…"

"But that's not the most important reason you want to stay." He finally had his dad face on, the one she could relate to, the person she loved so much because he understood her. "You sure?"

"It's more than the study or potentially helping catch the murderers. Sharon's still missing. What if she was abducted because they thought she was me? That's on my head. Oh, don't you give me that look that it's your fault. No. You've warned me for years to be aware and on my toes, one step ahead of anything like this. I let my guard down, Dad. I feel so selfish—"

"It's okay, Andrea. This isn't anyone's fault except the men with no thought to human life. I completely understand why you need to stay here. I'll explain everything to your mother. But we do this my way. When my team is ready. Make everyone believe you're here only to finish your thesis. No one knows the truth except my liaison."

She remembered Pete's arm around Mrs. Griggs, wondering who the liaison would be. If not Pete, then she'd be forced to act like a selfish, spoiled woman with no thought for anyone else other than herself, lying to Pete.

"My men said the Hiller was a piece of trash.

That was some nice flying this afternoon. Reminds me of our Sunday afternoon flights. That was a lot of years ago."

"Yes, sir. I miss them."

"We'll have to do it again sometime soon." He squeezed her hand. The closest thing to a hug she'd ever get in public.

"It's a date."

"For the record, I'm damn proud of you, Andrea. Very proud. And regarding the attempted abduction, you touched on several points that had already been considered by my team. They believe they're going to try again as another distraction. I'll be couriering a pair of earrings to you. Wear them at all times and I'll be able to find you."

They walked from the spare office and witnessed Logan's parents leaving.

"You don't have to do this." Her father spoke quietly, hope apparent in his voice. "You don't owe anyone anything."

"Yes, I do. For them, for Sharon and especially for me."

"Only one person will know the real reason you're staying. He'll be fully briefed and ready to move without my permission. You and I both will have to trust him with your life. I'll assign him to be in charge of your protection detail, but you can't tell him why you're really staying here. You can't tell anyone."

"I want Pete to be in charge."

"He's already declined my offer."

"I know that won't stop you. It would look more realistic for the sheriff to be in charge."

"I should lock you up and throw away the key."

She nodded and her father left her standing at the edge of the office. More like on the edge of reality. She couldn't believe she'd insisted on putting her life on the line. Something these men and women did daily.

Homeland Security. Texas Rangers. Drug Enforcement Administration. Presidio County Sheriff's Department. Pete would be another valued member of their new task force. But her role? She was the bait. She felt every bit exposed as if she were dangling midair on a small hook, holding on for dear life but her fingers were slipping.

Andrea was determined to stay, determined to help find Sharon, determined to put the creep behind all this confusion in jail. And like it or not, she was determined to find out why Sheriff Pete Morrison had no future.

It was a shame that to accomplish her goal she had to let him think her a selfish human being.

"I NEED TO speak with you, Sheriff Morrison," Commander Allen commanded, but remained outside the office.

No choice. He'd already received a phone call from the mayor ordering him to help in any capacity. He was sunk, but at least Andrea would be returning with her father and remain safe.

"Did they find your hat?" she asked out of the blue.

He was certain she had a look of mischief, just a slight tilt to those luscious lips and a twinkle in her eyes.

"I didn't check, but someone brought back the Tahoe. I imagine it'll turn up."

"This picture is great." She pointed to one his dad had caught of him shoving his hat on his head. "It'd be a shame to lose that hat."

"Andrea—"

"Were you on duty?"

"What? Oh, in the picture? No. I'd just been pitched from a bucking bronc at a local rodeo. Can you wait with Peach till I can get a protection detail together to take you back to the observatory?"

"I don't mind at all. The Commander actually threatened to arrest me to get me home. Fortunately, we came up with another arrangement. I want to help find Sharon. To do that, I had to concede to his terms. And if you're in here, that means he's given in to mine."

"What terms?"

"I hope you can forgive me, Pete. It really is the only way, but I'm not picking up my things and running home."

He was afraid to ask, and for some idiotic reason he felt like he'd been waylaid. He crossed his arms over his chest and backed to the door, wishing he had his hat brim to hide behind. "What terms?"

"I'm trusting you with my daughter's life," the Commander said through the doorway.

Why would her father state that she was leaving only to give in to Andrea's demands moments later? A quick glance at the enthusiasm on his dad's face, then a sharp stare at the woman who couldn't meet his eyes. A sliver of secretiveness was still there no matter how much she tried to hide it. And no matter how good an opportunity this sounded, Pete didn't think he would like working for her father.

She still hadn't answered his question. "One more time, Andrea. What terms?"

Victory was displayed in her smile as she finally met his eyes. "I'm staying as long as you're my personal escort and that you agree I'll stay at your ranch when not at the observatory."

"You mean, glorified babysitter." He turned to Commander Allen. "You said she was leaving."

"She was—now she's not. She agreed to stay put at the observatory and in your home."

Not only was he responsible for her every move miles away in another county, but she was supposed to bunk at their ranch? Live with him?

"You're willing to bring me onto your team so you can order me to play bodyguard for your daughter? Seems like you could have just asked me to assign her a protection detail."

"I'm a bit surprised by Andrea's change of heart, but I assure you there's much more involved than protecting my daughter." Another couple entered the sheriff's office. "Looks like my state liaison is here. Please escort my daughter to the conference room, Sheriff. You're both needed for the briefing."

Pete recognized the Texas Ranger entering his building and directed to the office. The woman next to him looked completely out of place. With an expensive suit and heels that belonged on a television show—completely ridiculous and useless for West Texas.

"Commander Allen? Cord McCrea, Texas Rangers. Nice to meet you in person. Good to see you, Pete." He turned to the woman next to him. "This is Special Agent Beth Conrad, Drug Enforcement Administration."

"We've got the upstairs briefing room cleared out and ready to go."

Everyone turned toward the stairs, with the exception of the woman in high-end heels. "Where's the elevator, please?"

"I'll show you the way," his father said, draping her arm over his.

When everyone except Andrea had left, he asked, "Why?"

She shrugged and averted her eyes. "I need to finish my thesis. If you're too busy for this opportunity I'm dropping in your lap, you can always ask your father to take on the job."

"That's not the reason I said no. You aren't safe here."

His new charge was hiding something and he had a really bad feeling he knew what it was.

Chapter Fifteen

Andrea followed the others upstairs to a vacant briefing room since Joe's old office was no longer big enough. Each person grabbed a chair and made introductions. Pete crossed his arms and leaned against the wall instead of taking the empty seat next to her.

The Commander was back in full force and sitting at the head of the table, definitely in charge. "I'm keeping this task force small for a reason. I would prefer we stay under the radar and not let our enemy know we're searching for him."

They all glanced in her direction, except Pete. "I'm not going to blab about it."

"We know. At approximately 2200 hours Friday evening, a severely beaten man came from the desert and—"

"If I may, Commander." Pete pulled his notebook from his back pocket. "McCrea and I are pretty familiar with this area. It might help to hear a detailed account of events."

"Then we're all up to speed. Sounds good," McCrea said.

The woman from the DEA compressed her lips and took out an electronic notepad.

"Andrea Allen was at the Viewing Area on Highway 90. People stop and watch for the lights to appear this direction—" he pointed to a spot on the map hanging behind him "—southwest toward the Chinati Mountains. A trucker reported seeing the lights at 2204. Andrea returned to her vehicle searching for a camera."

The camera. What had happened to it? She needed to ask her father, or maybe Joe would know. Pete recited the details of their adventure. She rubbed her wrist, which was still sore from all the climbing she'd done to escape that supply closet. She couldn't remember how she'd kept her wits to find her way out of the building. His mention of how she'd escaped got her a nod from both the Ranger and the DEA agent.

"Which brings us back to Commander Allen," Pete concluded. He remained standing and didn't look at her.

"The man who had been beaten was Lyle Moreland. He was one of mine. Trained to fly just about anything. McCrea had given us a tip that a new gang could be using helicopters to move drugs. We know that this has been done before, but whoever's in charge of this new group is smart and, unfortunately, patient."

"Did you know about this, Dad?" Pete asked.

"Not until I went to the car accident and met the Homeland crew."

"While you were there, did anyone find the observatory's video camera?" she asked quietly.

"Did you manage to record part of the altercation or anything Moreland might have said?" the DEA agent asked from across the table.

"I remember turning it on. Then he was there and unconscious."

"I didn't see it," Pete answered. Their fathers shook their heads.

"Perhaps that's why they believe Miss Allen knows something of importance," Agent Conrad surmised.

Andrea had just come to that same conclusion while waiting for a break to ask about the camera. The statement carried more weight with a real agent stating it as a possibility. Andrea knew how these things worked. It was like dealing with four "commanders." Only four because Joe watched them all chat, too.

Pete wanted answers as to why his department hadn't been included. The Ranger said, "Need-to-know basis." Pete seemed to keep his cool but didn't let the conversation end.

She quietly scooted her chair from the table. If she could get out of the room, she wouldn't have to lie about her real reason for staying in the area. She made it to the hallway without anyone asking her to take her seat again.

"Need a cup of coffee?"

"Oh, Joe. You scared me. Yes, I'd love a cup."

"I'm thinking you haven't had anything to eat. Want a bite, too?"

"No, thank you. I better hang around for my dad and I need to find a ride to the observatory."

"Pete's taking care of that."

"But—"

"No need to argue. He's already made up his mind. Tahoe's gassed and sitting out front." He waved his hand and started walking away but turned around, waving her closer to him and farther from the door. "There's a solid reason he believes he can't get involved with anyone. You should ask him. He might even tell ya."

Joe dropped this statement into her lap and headed down the stairs.

How did the man know that she'd overheard any portion of their conversation? It didn't really matter. Any connection with Pete would be based on the lies she promised to tell. After all this was over, he'd find out the truth and really have no reason to become involved with her. No matter how determined she'd been an hour ago, his reasons were none of her business. Period.

PETE NOTICED THE moment Andrea had crept out of the conference room. He wanted to stop the discussion, to follow her, but his dad had given him a thumbs-up and taken that job on himself.

Half an hour later she was still on a bench in the hallway. She might even be asleep.

"So we're agreed on a plan?" Commander Allen flattened his palms on the table, ready to push up out of the chair.

"Yes," everyone confirmed. Pete nodded his agreement.

He would funnel information to the Commander and the DEA through McCrea—who also had an informant in Presidio on the border. And as he'd been warned earlier, he'd been assigned the duty of keeping the witness safe. Although he'd never promised that he'd be with Andrea 24/7, he had agreed to provide her with a protection detail.

Beginning with him.

It was going to be a long night.

"Wondering if you should wake her?" her father asked from just behind him. He placed a hand on Pete's shoulder. "The answer would be yes. Back to that dang observatory and searching the stars for who knows what. Her mother can't understand her passion but I do. I was in the program at NASA for several years while she was growing up."

"You wanted to be an astronaut?"

"Damn right. Didn't you?"

"Afraid I wasn't at the top of my class." Close enough, but studying had never been his thing. "Are you staying the night, sir?"

"I did everything right, still didn't make it to space." Regret passed quickly over his face. "I'm confident that you've got this under control."

"You mean McCrea."

"I know who I meant." He patted his shoulder in a fatherly fashion and passed through to the hallway. "Andrea, time to get a move on."

"You leaving?" she said midyawn.

Pete went downstairs, collected messages and checked out an extra shotgun. He secured everything in the Tahoe, including the fast food Peach had ordered during the meeting. A government vehicle pulled up next to him. The driver was on his phone and stayed behind the wheel.

"Thanks for the eats."

"I told Brandie to double your usual and put it on your tab. You know, one of these days you're going to have to learn how to cook."

"Peach, you know dang well I haven't been home since Thursday. When would I have had time to cook?"

"I'll let my book club know you're ready for some casseroles. Looks like you're going to need them with company at your house."

"Lord save me from a death by casseroles." *And a frustrating woman living in the guest room.* He put his hands together in prayer just in time for Andrea and her father to enter the hallway.

The Commander shook Pete's hand, then took

his daughter's between his own before saying good-night and leaving.

Andrea turned to Pete. "Well, what now, Sheriff? Where's the escort?"

"You sure about this? I could catch your father before he pulls away. You were ready to leave with him this morning. I'm not certain I understand what's changed."

"Do you have a ride for me or not?"

"Right this way."

Five minutes down the road, he thought she'd given up the battle to stay awake again. Catching a nap before she worked all night seemed to be a good idea. He reached in his bag and pulled out a hamburger.

"That smells absolutely delicious."

"There's one for you."

He heard the bag rustle.

"Oh, my goodness. That's awesome. Thanks for thinking about me."

"Peach took care of it."

"Okay. Be sure and thank her for me," she said with her mouth full.

"I'll need to know your routine when we get there. And I need your word you won't vary from it."

"I promise. No playing, no hikes, no exception. Just straight to and from the telescope."

"I'm in charge of scheduling your escorts and protection. No one has authorization to make changes and I won't send a message via anyone else to do so.

Not even my father. Is that clear? If you don't hear it from me, you can assume the message is bogus."

"That works."

Her tone was short and abrupt. She acted mad at him, but for what? She'd actually called *him* spoiled when she was the one using her father's position, demanding to stay to finish her research. But what did he know? They'd kissed a few times. He didn't know anything about her.

There hadn't been time for much else. And there wouldn't be. He hadn't just been spouting words that she deserved a man with a future to his dad to shut him up. Without his job, he'd work their ranch with the few cattle they currently had. They couldn't keep the place up just on his dad's retirement. Hiring out as a ranch hand was his best option to help make ends meet.

But right now he had a job to do. Get Andrea to the observatory and ensure her safety until she left next week. He could do that and do it well. She didn't have to like him.

"What's so important about watching a star?" he asked. His curiosity had gotten the better of him. "What made you change your mind about leaving?"

"I'm working with a University of Texas astronomer who verified the most distant galaxy in the universe using several telescopes. For me this study is more about securing time with the actual telescope than studying the stars. If I finish my thesis and publish, I'll have a good chance of obtaining a position with one of the best telescopes in the world."

"This is about a job you may or may not get?"

"The Chilean Giant Magellan Telescope will begin construction soon and will have nearly five times the light-gathering power of the best infrared in the world. We'll see more distant galaxies and watch stars being formed. Someday I'd love to get on a team studying reionization."

Under different circumstances he'd appreciate the enthusiasm in her voice, the excitement displayed through her hands as she spoke of something she truly loved. Another time he'd ask her what all that meant. At the moment, he was confused.

"You're willing to risk your life, not to mention the men on your protection detail, for a potential job? And you called me selfish." *You're an idiot, Morrison!* He could keep his distance without insulting her.

"You asked about my work. I…um…understand that Logan is dead and Sharon is still missing. I can't change any of that."

"*You* could be missing. Do you understand that?"

"Yes, I do," she admitted quietly.

Then it hit him. "Son of a gun, your father stated three separate times that you were a witness and not an active member of the task force. You're both lying. Aren't you?"

"I'm staying at the observatory to finish my study."

"And hoping that those maniacs will try to get to

you again. Dammit." He hit the steering wheel hard enough to make his palm sting. "This is a stupid plan. I can't stand guard twenty-four hours a day."

"You aren't supposed to. They won't make a move if you're too close."

There it was, the admission. He was right and she was staying behind to draw the murderers out.

He jerked the car to the side of the road as soon as there was room to safely do so. "We're going back. Or I'm taking you to Alpine to catch the first flight to Austin. You can't go through with this. You have no idea what you're doing."

"You'd be surprised, but it doesn't matter. You don't have a say in the decision."

"Andrea," he beseeched, hoping her name and his tone could say more than the words that wouldn't form into sentences.

The closeness between them was strained. She'd pulled away after spending time with her dad. He knew why he had distanced himself, but why had she changed?

The soft gleam from the dashboard lights gave her a glow like one from a full moon. Perfect for someone who worked with the stars. He wanted to take her in his arms. Their attraction had them both leaning toward each other, until bright headlights interrupted and they both pulled back.

"I appreciate your concern, but I have to do this." She retreated as far as possible, wrapping her arms around herself like she was freezing to death. "This was my idea, Pete. But the Commander's superiors agree. Please believe me. Even my father's respecting my decision."

The nonstop nervous chatter he'd grown accustomed to had disappeared. This woman seemed completely in control. He faced forward, ready to continue to the observatory, wanting to know why it was so important to her yet holding back.

"You're right. It's not my call." Easing the vehicle back onto the empty road, he wanted to ask but couldn't allow himself to get closer to her. "Aw, hell, mind sharing why your dad insisted you weren't involved? Or why he wants the very task force he formed out of the loop?"

"It's better this way. Less chance of word getting out that it's a trap."

"I see. He said a couple of times that he didn't think you'd be part of the equation again. So no one's supposed to know except Cord. He knows, right?"

"Yes. Please don't think badly about my dad. He understands why I need to stay. Sharon's still missing, and if there's the slimmest chance…"

"I need to assign you a larger protection detail."

"No. Please, Pete." She leaned toward him. Close enough for him to see the strain on her face. "I have to do this."

"Not at the expense of losing your life."

"Again, it's not your call. If you refuse to help,

then you're not part of the loop. You can step away, and we'll get the Jeff Davis County sheriff to help."

"Over my dead body you will."

"Nothing that extreme, please. Like I told my dad, I promise I won't make any detours. Straight to work. Straight back to your ranch. I won't ditch my guard or anything like that. But if there's a chance that Sharon's alive and they still think I have some information, I need to be here to help."

"I admire your determination and courage, even if I think you're insane for volunteering to do this."

"Thanks, I think."

He'd already planned to handpick her protection detail from both counties. He'd already spoken with his father about driving her and made arrangements for the house to be cleaned. It would be a pain driving her back and forth, but he didn't care.

Nothing would happen to Andrea on his watch. They might not have a future together, but she definitely had places to go and stars to discover.

Chapter Sixteen

The operation had lost one helicopter and five men. Patrice would be upset. More accurately, her employer would be angry. Indeed, she was due here any moment. He uncorked her favorite California wine to let it breathe.

Homeland Security's spy had stolen from him and had the power to bring down more than what Patrice had lost. He was certain Andrea Allen had been given information at her car in the desert—whether she knew it or not.

Tomas had been too inquisitive. His intelligence should have given him away immediately as an undercover agent. But to his credit, he'd kept himself in the background operations for months. Unfortunately, their methods hadn't been able to obtain how he was making contact with DHS to pass any information back to his superiors.

If they hadn't learned of Miss Allen's importance, they might never have ferreted out the spy. He still wanted the young woman. Having her in his control was key to the next phase of operations.

It had been highly improbable Patrice's men would succeed in the abduction but well worth the try. The benefits far outweighed the losses. He heard the front door open.

"Miss Orlando, please come in."

"I told you it wouldn't work, Mr. Rook." She dropped her purse on the floor and stripped off her jacket, tossing it haphazardly across a brocade chair. She saw the wine, tilted some into a glass and gulped the fine red elixir too fast.

"Yes, you did." He bit his tongue to remain pleasant. "But I also informed you that it didn't matter to me what the cost was to you. The trucks made it into Manuel Ojinaga and we're on schedule."

"I'll need compensation for the men I've lost. Replacing them will cost me a bundle. I don't want to dip into my reserve, drawing attention to myself."

"Naturally. These men will be worth the higher price. Unless you'd like to reconsider?"

His fingers caught her exposed throat as she tossed back the last of the wine in the glass. She choked—partly on the wine, partly from the pressure of his grasp. The fragile handblown wineglass shattered on the floor. He should have waited until she'd set it on the table. Her fingers curled around his own, attempting to pry them away from her skin.

As her oxygen waned, her eyes grew enormous as she realized he controlled whether she lived or died. He saw the acknowledgment in her face, in the desperation of her clawing hands and kicking feet. Her dress rose to show the tops of her stockings.

Had she worn them for him today? Sex with her might be a satisfying distraction while he waited. He released his grip, immediately turning his back to give her a moment to recover.

As he was concentrating on board three, his next move presented itself. "Aw, thank you, Patrice. Nc6 is a very nice move."

She coughed and sputtered behind him, then began tugging on her dress. Yes, it was time to re-mind her who was in control. He gathered her things and offered his hand to help her stand.

"I'm in the mood to postpone the doldrums of business for a while. How about you?"

The fright in her eyes spurred his movements. He controlled himself, restraining from pulling her along. He glanced at the six boards, committing the pieces to memory. Ready to be inspired while Patrice was at his fingertips.

He opened the door, waving off his assistant. "Delay dinner an hour. Oh, wait, Mr. Oscuro."

Patrice's stylish dress had a visible zipper down the back. He'd noticed straightaway that she was also braless underneath. It had been a long while since he'd reminded her where her place was. He jerked her to a halt in the hallway, tugged the zipper and waited to see if she'd let the dress fall.

A small gasp of surprise was her only protest, and he'd let her have it. She dropped her arms to her sides and the dress amassed around her ankles with a gentle tug over her hips. He offered his hand again to help her step over the sleek red pile. She took it. The bruises on her shoulder and neck visible against her flawless skin.

"Marvelous. Simply marvelous. That's all, Oscuro."

He nodded to the near-naked woman. She brought a smile to his lips like no other could. But she needed to know he'd sacrifice her faster than a knight's pawn if she defied him or took his courtesy for granted.

Chapter Seventeen

There's a solid reason he believes he can't get involved with anyone. You should ask him.

Andrea tried to work on entering new information into her database. She'd managed to eke out a couple of sentences on her dissertation during the past two hours. Useless. Her mind kept coming back to Joe's statement and wondering why he couldn't just tell her what the reason was himself.

"This is hopeless." She shut the laptop lid and rubbed her aching eyes. All her things had been moved to the Morrison ranch house, but she still had her assigned room at the dormitory where she could work. She'd come early today, hoping to get caught up without any distractions.

Distractions like Pete sleeping in the next room or working horses in the late afternoon. Yesterday from her window she'd seen him thrown from a horse. She'd wanted to run to him to make sure he was okay. Willpower hadn't stopped her. She'd been frozen to the windowsill watching him take off his shirt to shake out the dirt.

So she'd come to the observatory early in order to avoid those type of incidents today.

Studying, applying herself or stringing words together for a paper had never been a problem...until now. She'd never had trouble sleeping at odd hours before. You got used to that when you studied the stars. Who was she kidding? Sleep deprivation had nothing to do with it. Every thought centered on Pete and the cryptic advice his father had given her.

Just concentrate.

Three nights watching the farthest regions of the galaxy and she couldn't type up her notes. Learning the nuances of the 9.2 meter mirror on the telescope hadn't relieved her or excited her the way it usually did. And if she did manage to keep on track for a few minutes, the next person entering the room would ask her about the shooting or share how she and Pete had escaped. Or they'd tell her what they were doing during the shooting. She'd either commend them or apologize to them.

During the day, construction crews were down the hill at the Visitor Center repairing windows and bullet holes. The shattered glass had been swept up and thrown away. Pete's dad had tried to capture her would-be abductors alive, but they'd all chosen to fight to the death. One had escaped into the woods and been tracked for several hours until he also stepped in front of a bullet.

The manhunt was the reason authorities had delayed searching for them after she'd landed the

Hiller chopper in the middle of nowhere. It was ridiculously hard not to think about the incident. Much harder not to think about Pete.

Her hands smoothed the laptop. Was she ready to open it and get serious? *No.* She wanted to stop thinking of Pete. Andrea stepped out of the main room of the dormitory.

"Hi, Bill. Need anything?" She spoke to the guards throughout each day, making a point to learn the names of the men who accepted the risk of protecting her.

Pete had warned the deputies not to take the assignment for granted. Joe reminded them each morning when dropping her off at the ranch about potential attacks. He stressed the danger without disclosing specifics about the task force or possible trap they could be setting.

"No, thanks, Andrea," Bill answered, tipping his hat and resuming his watch.

The crime scene and repairs had closed the main building and classroom. Neither was necessary for the star parties. From out here she could see the visitors lining up on the sidewalk, claiming their telescopes. It would be a beautiful night for stargazing.

The observatory was short on staff and volunteers. She'd received an email asking for all volunteers to help with the class tonight. Her telescope was set and she wasn't needed until much later. Why not help?

There was no reason other than writing or compiling data. If she wasn't going to do either of those, then she could give back a little. After all, she was the reason all the windows were broken.

Technically, she'd promised not to do anything other than study at the observatory and sleep at Pete's ranch. The Commander had forced a promise and then Pete had asked for one. But it had been two full days and three nights without another person making an untoward move against her.

The closed spaces were beginning to make her twitch. She needed to move, feel a little free.

Wasn't volunteering to help kids considered part of her job? She'd helped a couple of times her first week and loved it. The star parties were so much fun and, man, oh, man, she needed some fun. It wasn't like getting in her car and driving into town. She would still be at the observatory and keeping her promise.

She pulled on tennis shoes and practically ran down the hill from her dormitory room. Bill stayed close after jumping into his squad car and repeating ten times that she needed to wait. She slowed and took a deep breath of the crisp clean air as she got closer to the café patio and where Pete had been shot.

Last Friday afternoon, she'd taken the same walk to get to Sharon's car. On that journey she hadn't nearly been killed in a car accident, shot at on the observatory patio, stranded in the mountains or kissed by a sheriff. The very same sheriff who seemed to avoid her as often as possible.

His days were full of work—doubly so since he'd joined the task force. Her days were full of sleep. Her nights were busy with calculations and stars. His were surrounded by dreams. At least she hoped they were.

Stubborn man.

Right now, this very minute, was about sharing her love for the stars. Helping someone—child or adult—find a constellation or a crater on the nearly full moon.

There's a solid reason he believes he can't get involved with anyone. You should ask him. Joe's words orbited around in her mind like a moon around its planet. They were constantly there with no choice but to continue.

The next time she saw the sheriff of Presidio County...she was going to ask.

"THE SOURCE IS RELIABLE. They're going to use the cover of the UFO Border Zone to move something major." Cord McCrea had been trying to stop drug trafficking since transferring to West Texas almost ten years before. He knew the area and could get information from a dried cactus.

The men who had followed Andrea to the observatory had inside information—from either the police radio or bugged cell phones. So he met Cord in an open area dead cell coverage zone between their properties. Making certain their conversations weren't monitored or overheard. Pete wasn't taking a chance with Andrea's life. Not a second time.

"How would they use the UFO convention? It's not like there are crowds and crowds of people wandering everywhere. The thing draws a couple of thousand at best. And that's during the concerts. They've only been having the conference for a couple of years now." Pete caught himself shoving his hair back and resituating his hat. A habit Andrea had drawn to his attention when she'd arranged his hair with gel. His fingers had gotten stuck a couple of times in the stiff edges. After every shower now, he stopped himself when he reached for the styling tube.

"I don't know, Pete. All I can confirm is what my informant tells me. And that's all he's got."

"What's the deal with your task force? Do I need to be doing anything differently?"

Cord stretched his back. He'd been shot several years before by drug traffickers. All those men were behind bars or hadn't survived a second confrontation. "Naw. Just keep being the sheriff and keep Allen's daughter safe. You could let me know who you'll be sending to the aliens conference."

"You got it." Exactly what he'd thought. He'd been put on the task force only because of Andrea. "Cord, I know Andrea's being used as bait."

"I didn't think it would stay a secret from you long."

"Is that right? Why?"

Cord raised a curious eyebrow. "Come on, man. I saw the way you two looked at each other. The tension the other night could be cut with a knife. She insisted on staying at your place, having you as her protection detail. Allen wanted you in charge of the border detail."

So those were her terms.

Cord clapped him on the back. "I can see that brain of yours working, pal. That's right. Miss Allen wouldn't trust anyone else with her life. Just you. Go ahead, stick that chest out a little farther. Does that make you feel more important?"

They both laughed, but he did feel more competent.

"Just so you know, I'll be filling her in on our suspicions that something's happening. I want her to be prepared."

"Makes sense."

"Kate and the new baby okay? We haven't seen much of her around town."

"They stay close to the house, but they're great. Danver's a regular roly-poly. Kate's brother David is coming in at the end of the month, which is a code word for barbecue with the McCreas. Bring your dad."

"Sure. As long as this thing's over by then."

"You realize that we're never going to be done

with drug traffickers trying to make a buck. We stop this group, another one is standing right behind it ready to take up the reins and harness a new set of horses. It'll never be over," Cord said sadly.

"Job security. What more can a man ask for?" He shrugged. At least Cord had job security. The position of sheriff—no matter how competent Pete felt—might be out of the question for him.

"There's more to life, man. I hope you'll find out what soon." He tipped his hat. "See you around. I'll give you a holler if my guy comes through with more info about the shipment."

"I'll have additional deputies in or near Presidio. They were already on the schedule to be at the UFO conference. Hard to understand that's the date they're choosing…when we have *more* men posted there."

"My source is more reliable than they normally come. It ain't gospel, but it's close. Take care now." Cord closed the door of his truck and drove out on the broken trail.

Pete stayed put, leaning on his Tahoe, watching the first evening star shine in the darkening sky. Andrea would have been dropped off about an hour ago. His dad was driving her from the ranch to the observatory and a deputy would pick her up in the morning and drive her to the ranch.

He would have to talk to her sooner or later. They couldn't keep successfully avoiding each other. He finished his soda and crushed the can, tossing it into the back. A couple of minutes on the road and he could make a call.

"Dispatch, reassign the driver for Miss Allen in the morning. I'll be picking her up myself."

"You don't say," Peach answered. "I told Honey you'd come around."

"Thanks for the confidence."

"Well, we did raise you as a hero, not a coward."

"I'll be signing off now, Dispatch."

"'Night, Sheriff."

Not a coward. For the past three days, he sure as hell had been one where Andrea Allen was concerned. Dammit.

PETE WAVED AT Randy Grady still on his feet at the door where Andrea was working. "Didn't they have a chair for your shift?"

"I didn't want to get too comfortable and nod off. You said to stay on our toes. I thought your dad was picking up Miss Allen?" They shook hands.

"He had an errand this morning, so I'm filling in."

"How's the arm?"

Pete stretched it across his chest. "Surprisingly good."

"Heard you passed out." Randy snickered under his breath.

"More from a lack of sleep than this thing."

"Right." Randy sang a song as he said the one word, doubting. He trotted down the sidewalk and stopped. "She's a nice woman. Any chance this protective detail will be over before she blows town?"

"Don't think so. Not with her father."

"Totally understand. I'd keep her for myself, too. I'll head out, then."

"It's not like that." But at the back of his mind, he knew it was. Randy disappeared down the path, and Pete stopped himself from shouting a denial.

He watched the sky lighten in the east through the treetops. Andrea would be out any minute. Why had he decided to pick her up? The dare from Peach? He had nothing to prove. Andrea would be gone at the end of the week without a glance back in his direction.

She didn't need any of the complications that getting involved with him would bring. The door opened.

"Oh, hi," Andrea said, then waved behind her. "My ride's here, guys. See you tomorrow."

Pete scanned the perimeter, including the skyline for a possible chopper, avoiding eye contact with his assignment. There had been three days without a hint of an incident. None of the deputies had reported any unusual activity. No one had reported any unusual cars or visitors hanging around either Fort Davis or Marfa.

"I'm surprised to see you."

"Why?"

"Well, Randy was here earlier."

"He just left. I thought I'd give you a ride back to the ranch. Do you need anything else?"

"Nope, I've got everything." She patted her laptop bag. "Gorgeous morning."

"That it is." She was a step ahead of him. He could take a long, good look at her. Gone was the bandage around her wrist, and the bruise was fading. Tight-fitting jeans covered her slender figure. A McDonald Observatory souvenir T-shirt hugged a tiny waist, giving him a terrific view.

They both got inside the Tahoe, and he drove away from the observatory, watching for stalled cars or men on the road. He noticed Andrea's constant movement and glances behind them. "You seem kind of antsy. Something on your mind?" he asked after a few minutes.

"I was just waiting for you to drop the real reason you're personally picking me up. I know you've been avoiding me. Did something happen? Did they send a new threat?"

"Nothing like that. I thought I'd give you a chance to pick up anything you might need. Our schedules haven't been conducive for much socializing, that's all." *And let you know about the possible threat for the next three days.* But those words stuck in his throat.

"And whose fault is that?"

"I wouldn't place blame on anyone. It's just the way it happened to turn out." Peach's words argued with his conscience. If he did say something, what good would it do?

"So, did something happen? Do you have a message from my father?"

"Wouldn't Commander Allen be calling you directly?"

"I really don't know. This isn't exactly our normal situation. We normally don't talk that often."

"That's a downright shame."

Andrea laughed. "You've heard all about the educational differences I've had with my family. Now it's your turn to share."

"My dad and I get along just fine."

"You can't get off that easy. I've been living in your house. Joe's walking on eggshells and you guys barely say three words to each other."

"He had a heart attack, and I've sort of been busy."

"Oh, I know all about that. It's nothing to take lightly, but he's exercising and has lost seventeen pounds by changing his diet."

"How did you know that?"

"He brags about using a new belt hole all the time. You'd know if you were around him for more than five minutes. Is it the upcoming election? Are you afraid he's going to be upset that you're taking his job?"

The desire to spill everything to Andrea was tempting. In spite of the nonstop chatter and her irresistible kissing ability, she was easy to talk with.

He'd kept his dad's secret without saying a word for six weeks.

"I take your silence for a yes."

"Joe Morrison has been ready to retire. I know he'll miss the people, but he's been frustrated with the day-to-day stuff for a while now."

"He said you're running unopposed, so what's the problem? Why are you nervous?" she asked.

"You seem pretty cozy with my dad, but I'm not sure this is any of your business."

"What can I say? I like to talk."

"I've noticed."

"Are you mad at him because of me? I mean, Joe agreed to help the Commander. I know all this is an added strain. Especially having to drive me back and forth to the observatory."

"I have an idea. Why don't we listen to the radio and you take a break from thinking too hard on my problems."

"Okay, but I don't do country. Are there any classic rock stations around here?" Andrea turned away.

Pete immediately wanted to spill his guts. He'd been rude in order to stop himself from telling her everything. By the time they turned south into Fort Davis, he was ready to beg her to chatter again. He liked her voice and hadn't realized how much he'd missed it.

"You're right," he said, unable to take the silence.

At least she looked at him, eyebrows arched, waiting for him to continue.

"It's not…" Could he appease her curiosity without sharing all the details of his problem? No. In a very short time, this woman had gotten into his psyche. He wanted to be honest with her. But he just didn't know if he could be.

Telling anyone would be risking everything his dad had worked to achieve for thirty years.

"If things were different—" He clammed up… again.

"I get it. This is personal and I'm a stranger."

"Why is it so important to you?"

"You and your dad have been a big help this week. I owe you a lot. I hate to see your relationship strained because of me."

"It has nothing to do with you."

"Okay, I'd believe that. Except, after my dad formed this task force, you didn't want to have anything to do with me. And Joe said I should just ask you why. I would have sooner, but you made it pretty clear—"

"Wait a minute. Slow down. Dad told you to ask me why?"

"Yes, when he left the meeting Saturday, he said you had a good reason for acting like a jerk."

"He's called me worse."

Andrea turned a nice shade of embarrassed pink. "Sorry, that's actually my description. But you didn't even give me a chance to say thanks for saving my life before you completely brushed me off."

"I think we sort of saved each other. We made a good team."

"And that has to end?"

He took the vehicle through Marfa and made the last couple of turns to the ranch without responding.

"Look, Andrea, I don't see the point. You'll be on a military chopper out of here in four days. I have no doubts your father will keep you as far away as he can from Marfa, Texas, and this drug cartel. After that, you're trying to get a job on the other side of the world."

"Oh, so that's it. You're afraid of short-term relationships. Have you been burned before?"

He pulled past the front of the house, waving to his dad on the front porch. The grin and waggling eyebrows on his dad's face were enough of a sign that everything appeared normal. He parked, cut the engine and got a strange feeling his dad expected something to happen with Andrea and him.

She unbuckled, turning his direction. A playful grin replaced the serious expression from earlier. "I got the impression from the nurses the other night that you were a popular guy."

"Popular? I've had a few dates, nothing serious—"

"Hold that thought. Do you hear something?" She opened her door and hopped out before he could react. "Is that a helicopter? Was it following us?"

He drew his weapon as he jumped from the Tahoe, searching, seeing nothing. Andrea continued to the far side of the barn, her face turned to the sky.

"Wait! Don't run out in the open! Dammit, exactly like what you're doing."

Chapter Eighteen

Andrea ran until she got a good look at the helicopter heading away from the ranch. A sense of relief that their day wouldn't be interrupted swept over her as fast as the pleasant northern breeze. She stopped, and a second later, Pete skidded to a halt behind her. He stretched out his arms to steady her but quickly dropped them to his sides.

"Still alive." She shrugged. Hopefully indicating that running had been the wrong thing to do. "We don't have to make a big deal out of this, Pete. I know I shouldn't run off like that. It won't happen again."

"When am I supposed to make a big deal out of it? After they succeed in abducting you?"

Andrea was tired of seeing Pete's face worried instead of smiling. In the past few days, when that deep furrow appeared across his brow it was because of her. She was also tired of avoiding her attraction. Deep down, she knew that part of the reason she'd stayed in the area was her attraction to this man.

There was just something about him. Something sweet about his silence, though he was strong to his core. She wanted to discover what centered him and made him so easily confident without conceit. Simply put…she wanted to know him better.

So it made perfect sense to kiss him again.

"Did I finally ask something you don't have an answer for?"

Shrugging a little, she couldn't help smiling at the confusion in Pete's eyes. His hat was already in his hand or she might have pushed it off his head to the ground. He took a step back. She followed with two steps, catching his shoulders. With one small twist, she had him next to the barn wall.

He knew what was coming. She knew because his head tilted sideways and his face dropped even with hers.

"This is a bad idea, Andrea."

"You've got to have a better reason."

There was a hairbreadth between their lips. They stayed there, taking in each other's air. The minty clean made her wish she'd taken him up on the lifesaver he'd offered in his car. His chest began to rise and fall quicker, matching hers. His hands tightened around her waist, and she draped hers around his shoulders.

"Bad, bad idea," he said before crushing his lips to hers.

Sheriff Pete Morrison might think kissing her was a bad idea, but the man hauling her hips to his... Well, he left nothing but good sensations behind.

"The suggestion that any part of this is bad...absolutely ridiculous," she whispered close to his ear. "You are such a good kisser."

"You make me crazy," he said. He smashed his mouth to hers again, not allowing her to respond.

The returning kiss she gave him should have been answer enough. She was desperate not to let him go this time. Her body needed him, and his needed her.

She pulled back, dipping her mouth, tasting the salt on his skin, nipping the curve where his shoulder muscle met his neck. She tilted her head back, encouraging him to taste the V of her throat, sending additional shivers of anticipation down her spine.

His lips traveled down her breastbone, lightly scraping his teeth across her sensitive skin. His tongue darted under the lacy edge of her bra. His hands stretched along her sides, then tugged at her T-shirt, making her wish she'd worn the button-up hanging in her bedroom.

Oh, gosh, a bedroom would be nice. They could take their desire to the next level. But they couldn't... They weren't alone. But that didn't stop the exploring.

Pete's cool hands slid under her shirt, up her back and to her sides. He skimmed her breasts, just the thin lace separated the tips of his fingers and her flesh.

More shivers. At this rate there would be endless shivers and no relief in sight. She wanted his shirt off, but it was firmly tucked into his pants. She settled for skimming the tops of his ears, dragging her nails gently across his scalp and filling her hands with his thick hair.

Pete caught her mouth to his again, plunging his tongue inside. He captured her whimper as their hips gnashed together again. Wanting more than either could deliver in broad daylight on the side of the Morrison barn.

"Ahem." Joe cleared his throat from the corner of the barn.

Breathing too hard to speak, Andrea looked in his direction and could only see the toe of one boot and a long, tall shadow.

Breathing a little hard himself, Pete dropped his forehead just above her ear. Then he whispered, "Very bad idea."

"Not at all," she whispered back, noticing his hands settled on her hips, his thumbs comfortably hooked inside her jeans.

"Um, son. Since you're going to be here with our guest, I thought I'd take Rowdy into town. We need feed and supplies. I have a few errands. We'll probably be gone a good three or four hours, so I thought we'd grab lunch at the café."

"You don't have—"

She placed a finger over Pete's lips, fearing he'd convince his father not to leave. She lowered her voice again. "I promise to be good…and not run away."

Pete dropped his head against the barn, then his eyes seared her with their heat. "Fine, Dad. I got this covered."

Yes, he did.

PETE NEEDED TO drop his hands and lock the county's guest in her bedroom. That would be the right thing to do. The responsible thing. The sheriff thing. He could try. But the way his body was throbbing it would take every ounce of control he no longer had.

Holding Andrea in his arms, he'd lost control. If his dad hadn't interrupted them, there was no telling what he would have done. His heart rate was still thrumming at top speed. If he didn't have a grip on her hips, his hands would be shaking.

The horn from the truck sounded a couple of blasts. A minute later he heard it leaving. He stayed put, reluctant to let Andrea go because he knew what needed to be done.

"We should get inside." He reluctantly dropped his hands, pressing them against the barn.

Andrea stepped to the side and picked up his hat. She handed it to him, then put her fists on her slim hips. "What's wrong? You embarrassed?"

He shoved his hat on his head and circled her

wrist, tugging a little to get her started. "Inside and no. Or yes, a little."

Once they were around the corner and headed to the house, she twisted her wrist free. "I've been walking on my own for a while now."

"Come on, Andrea. You're under my protection. We can't— I shouldn't let my guard down or take advantage of our situation." He opened the screen door, ready to let her go through and plant himself on the porch until his father returned.

Looking him up one side and down the other, she seemed to read his mind and paused. To add to his misery, she took a seat on the porch swing and gestured for him to join her.

The chain suspending the swing creaked above their heads in a gentle rhythm as they sat shoulder to shoulder, silent. The horses clopped around in the corral. The breeze was picking up and blowing the top branches in the tree. Then just like high school, Pete found his hand inching toward Andrea's, then lacing their fingers together.

"This is nice. My mom would love this porch. She'd decorate it with all sorts of plants and small statues. She loves statues." She didn't seem mad.

In fact, she seemed to be in a great mood. Just like before their make-out session. Man, she was completely different from any woman he'd ever met. Shouldn't she be furious with him instead of holding his hand, sending lightning bolts up his arm or making small talk?

"Plants don't do so well out here in the winter." He could make small talk and ignore the energy surging through his body at her touch. Could he ignore that they had the house to themselves for the next three hours?

"Your dad is convinced that your reason for halting a potential relationship between the two of us is *solid*, as he put it. I, on the other hand, am not convinced."

So much for small talk.

"I have a lot of good reasons." It was easier to remember they couldn't be together when he wasn't touching her. He just couldn't force himself not to enjoy the smoothness of her skin. In fact, the memory of her incredible breasts made it hard to keep his seat.

"Why can't you tell me, Pete?"

"It's complicated."

"Then why is your dad so eager for you to share these reasons?"

"I don't know."

"One more question and then I'll go to my room." She looked down, dragged her toes and stopped the swing.

"Go for it."

"I think I will." She arched those beautiful brows again and winked. "Does it really matter for the next three hours?"

Chapter Nineteen

Pete watched Andrea's eyes slowly look into his and with his free hand, he tilted her chin until he could brush her lips again. Close enough to share her breath, her softness and her taste, and still far enough apart to quit. All he had to do was release her hand and let her go.

"What about all your reasons?" she asked.

His mind raced to find one legitimate objection not to finish what they'd started.

They'd only known each other a few days. That wasn't cause enough to stop. He felt drawn to Andrea like he'd known her all his life. And he wanted to know her better. Completely.

He wanted to taste the rest of her, working his way down from her slightly salty neck to her cute little toes. He wanted to find out if she was ticklish behind her knees or at the curve above her hip. He wanted to keep her to himself for a week of Sundays and forget the rest of the world and his list of reasons.

He didn't have a future. Hell, she only wanted three hours. The way his body was humming, he could guarantee that short time would be a long unforgettable adventure.

He was in charge of her protection. Her father working with Border Protection and Homeland Security still wasn't enough to make him stop. He'd take his chances.

But could the biggest reason on his list be ignored? *He was a phony.* He didn't want to lie to her, but it wasn't his secret. No matter how much she liked him, he couldn't take a chance telling anyone. Ever.

Pete stood quickly and jerked her into his arms. Her blue eyes were a perfect match with the sky. A perfect backdrop to kiss her again. He wanted to consume her, but he managed to keep his hands on her upper arms. He pressed his mouth to hers, coaxing her lips apart enough to enjoy the luxurious softness.

He wanted her with a fierce need that made nothing else matter. It had started in the hospital with each cheeky answer she'd given to his questions. And he honestly didn't see an end happening soon. It would, just not today. He'd already wasted enough of her remaining time in town. He tapered off their kiss in order to coax her to the door.

Andrea curved her hips into his, leaning back as she'd done on the far side of the barn. Her smile was sultry, sexy. "Does this mean you've changed your mind about the next three hours?"

With her looking like that at him, they weren't going to make it to the bedroom.

PETE KISSED HER hard and wrapped his arms around her waist as she wrapped hers around his neck. He moved toward the door, almost dragging her feet across the porch as he lifted her body next to his. Andrea didn't care. She was in just as big a hurry. Give the man too much time to think and he might change his mind.

Their limbs tangled as they helped each other take off their shirts. Hers pulled straight over her head, while she could only get his unbuttoned. Still kissing and touching, they dashed down the hall to the bedrooms.

"Mine," she said, bouncing against the closed door and struggling to turn the knob.

Pete didn't object. He skimmed her black bra— thank goodness she'd worn the sexy one—then traced her collarbone, moving higher until he cupped her neck with one hand and opened the door with the other. They backed into her bedroom, lips frantically finding each other again.

The belt holding his holster was unlatched. Andrea shoved his uniform over his shoulders and tugged his undershirt loose. Her hands skimmed his chest, hot flesh against her palms.

She returned his hard, deepening kisses, breaking long enough to stretch the white cotton over his head and let it fall to the floor. His hands slid down her back and seconds later her bra fell. Pete took a step back, his eyes smoldering as they saw her for the first time. She paused, letting him, not feeling vulnerable or self-conscious.

Andrea couldn't pretend to be a shy girl. She wasn't. Neither could she act coy and tiptoe around what she wanted. She'd wanted Pete Morrison since noticing his dimples back in the hospital. And what girl wouldn't want to make out with the man responsible for saving her life, not just once but twice?

"This has to be the *best* bad decision I've ever made."

"Oh, yeah?" She reached for the button on his fly and couldn't miss his physical reaction to her body as she unzipped his pants. "Then why are we slowing down?"

"Some things are worth savoring."

The smolder in his eyes turned to pure flame, spreading the heat to his entire body. He held her, letting her arch her back over his arm as he kissed and nipped a hot trail to her breast. By the time he reached the second, he laid her on the bed, taking his time to explore.

Pete stood between her legs, which were still encased in the heavy denim. His strong hands glided slowly down her thighs. If she hadn't been going crazy with anticipation, she might have screamed for him to hurry. But the anticipation was exquisite as he undressed her, giving a final tug to the tight jeans.

"You are more than beautiful. I could stare at you like this all day."

"You better not. What's good for the gander is good for the goose, you know." She winked suggestively and scooted farther onto the bed, pointed at his pants and propped her head up for a more comfortable look. "Strip, mister."

"Yes, ma'am."

Without much effort, Pete divested himself of all clothing and stood at the side of the bed a second before he looked uncomfortable. But that was only for a second. He got onto the bed, leaning on his side, and worked magic with his hands again.

Feather-soft strokes up and down her breastbone sent tingles all over her body. He drew concentric circles until her nipples drew tight, making her shiver multiple times. The strokes became longer, including her hips and thighs. Then tiny circles at the back of her knees.

"You've got a gentle touch," she gasped a little before he created a trail up her body with his lips. Then silenced her again with decadent kissing.

Andrea eagerly explored Pete's body, too. His sinewy muscles, long powerful thighs, lean hips and sheer strength left her breathless. When he reached between their bodies, she grabbed his shoulders, unable to keep her nails from lightly scraping into his skin. Moments later, her body hummed in fleeting perfection as she cried out.

Pete rolled to his side next to her, kissing her along her shoulder up to her neck, following the line of her jaw back to her lips. There wasn't an inch of relaxed parts on the man as she reached out and explored more.

It took a slight nudge to reverse their positions. Seconds later, Pete was on his back. She rose to her knees, massaging his chest, admiring the muscles extending to his hips. She mimicked his technique of touch. She loved the fine dusting of manly hair on his legs, drew circles behind his knees, where he jerked away and laughed.

As much as she loved those dimples, another touch made him suck in his breath and tighten his abs. She shimmied up his body, her breasts sensitive as they flattened against his chest.

"I need my…my pants," he said, gulping air.

"Oh, no, you don't, mister. You aren't getting away now."

"Not…leaving." He smiled, pushing gently at her shoulders, then cupping her breasts, making her join him on a long sigh. Then he whispered, "Condom."

He groaned when she sat up, connecting them and then again when she left to retrieve his slacks. She tossed his wallet to him, repositioning herself across his thighs, hand extended for the foil packet. Once the condom was on, she was no longer in control. His smile was replaced with a look of longing.

His gentle, slow touch was replaced with a frenzy she could barely control. He flipped her to her back and filled her.

Their joining was more than she'd thought it could be. They settled into a rhythm that belonged only to them. It couldn't be duplicated with anyone else.

"Meant to be" kept repeating in her head. No words were needed and none were said as their lips opened for each other just like their bodies. The perfection she'd experienced at his touch shortly before returned in extended stellar abundance. Pete joined her, tossing back his head as his body went supernova.

Chapter Twenty

"Think you could tell me about your list of reasons now?" Andrea asked, her head nestled in the crook of his shoulder. Her body was only half covered with the sheet, so he could still admire her flawless skin and curves.

"I'd rather make love to you again before I go remembering why I shouldn't."

"Don't get all hot and bothered because you're my protection detail."

"That's easy for you to say. What am I supposed to write in the report?"

"You can say I spent a pleasant morning in my room. You don't really write everything down for my father, do you?"

He'd pass answering that question honestly because the answer had been yes until an hour ago. "So now you know the real reason why I've tried to talk us out of this."

She climbed on top of him, close enough to kiss, her breasts gently grazing his chest. "I really want to know, Pete. I meant what I said about staying in touch when I leave." She paused, her head cocking to the side with realization. "I thought you were kidding earlier about long-distance relationships. But you really don't want that."

He gently held her in place when she tried to roll away.

"Just hold your horses. Before you start rapid-firing questions off only an assumption. I never said I didn't want a relationship, close or long-distance."

"Then what is it? I can tell that something's bothering you. Is it my dad?" She turned her head again. "I knew it. The Commander is such a turnoff to potential boyfriends. But good grief, Pete. You're the sheriff. You can't possibly think he'll find out something about you…"

He couldn't look into her eyes. She was reading his mind—or doing a dang good job interpreting his expressions. She scooted to his side, pulling the sheet higher and tucking it around her like a toga. He threw his legs over the side of the bed.

And once again, Andrea surprised him with a comforting hand soothing his back muscles. She didn't seem indignant or curious. She just ran her fingertips lightly up and down, giving him a chance to think of what he should say.

"I should have just made love to you again."

She laughed and pressed her body to his, her arms lightly circling his neck. Her tongue flicked out enticingly against his earlobe.

"You don't have to tell me anything else," she whispered. "I'm very happy to take you up on your offer."

He twisted in her arms and dropped them both nose to nose on their sides.

"This isn't about you or your father, Andrea."

"All right. Since you don't know me very well, perhaps I should inform you that I'm pretty good keeping a secret. I once kept a secret for my best friend for almost two years. That actually might be because I forgot about it, but it should still—"

"Shh," he said just before covering her lips.

The long kisses kept them both silent. He wanted to tell her. She deserved to know that it had nothing to do with her. The frenzy slowed but not the intensity. Soon he was kissing his way down her body and loving every part of her.

"THAT WAS INSANE," Andrea said, collapsing next to Pete. "I can barely breathe. How much of our three hours is left?"

She'd fallen for Pete faster than a shooting star fleeted through the sky. And she was glad. He was a complex man, very intriguing and just plain adorable. Plus, he was a heck of a lover. A seriously wonderful lover. She had to be careful she didn't meet the same fate as a shooting star and burn up when it hit the atmosphere.

"Enough for a shower and breakfast." He was

propped on the pillows, the corner of the sheet modestly covering his vulnerable parts.

"You mean lunch," she teased.

"Or dinner if you look at the fact that we both worked all night and neither of us has slept in a while."

"Wow, Sheriff. You did all that on no sleep? I can't wait until you're functioning at full capacity." She laughed, but she was also impressed at how this man could be wide awake for just over thirty hours.

"Shower, food and sleep. In that order."

"Sounds like a plan. If I can move, that is. Maybe I'll just stay here for a couple of days and recover."

He pushed off the bed and she admired his backside as he gathered his clothes. "Race you."

"You're on. First one finished has to cook."

"I might have a better idea. We wash each other's backs, finish together and both cook." He caught her wrist and pulled her to him. His sexy definition of "cook" was pressed between them.

"I really am hungry," she said only because she'd noticed their time was running short. Otherwise she would have been all over the possibility of another romp. "Didn't Joe say they'd be back around one?"

"You're right. We'll save the shower for next time."

"I love a good plan of action." She winked at him as he patted her behind, then swaggered down the hallway.

He beat her out of the shower only because she

made certain her legs were shaved again. Who knew? They might actually get time alone together before heading to work. She slid the understated tracking devices back into her ears and yawned. They needed something upbeat to keep them alert, at least long enough to eat.

Music. Shoot, hers had been stolen. Well, at least the device had been kept by the men in the desert. Fortunately, all her music was stored electronically and could be accessed via Wi-Fi. She grabbed the university-issued tablet from her bag and followed the aroma of sizzling bacon.

"Oh, my gosh, that smells delicious." She got close to Pete, stealing a kiss when he faced her. She didn't want him to retreat to their relationship status prior to the front porch. So she stood right next to him, hoping the popping grease wouldn't reach her bare arms.

"Nothing fancy. I'm too tired for anything other than breakfast." He pulled her close, then let her back away from the frying pan.

"I don't mind. I'm starving." She suddenly wanted to know more about him. What could he cook? What did he like to eat? There were so many unanswered, frivolous details. The only conversations they'd had were about parents or Sharon or madmen who might still be trying to abduct her. She powered the tablet on and set it on the table. "Hey, what kind of music do you like? Are you a good ol' country boy? A hard rocker? Oh, please don't be a closet classical music guy. That might just be a deal breaker."

He threw his head back, laughing. She loved getting that reaction from him and watching those dimples. Spatula in hand, he drew her into the circle of his arms and just looked at her. She dropped her head onto his chest, hugging him.

"You are so lucky you're the sheriff."

"What do you mean?"

"Well, my dad's probably running an extensive background check on you, verifying that you're good enough to date his only child."

"Are you serious?" He broke their embrace faster than she could wonder what was happening. "He can't. You've got to ask him to stop."

"What's wrong?" She knew something major had changed. The smile had disappeared and was instantly replaced with a look so serious it frightened her.

"I like you, Andrea. Give your dad a call, will ya?"

"I like you, too. I know my dad can be a bit overwhelming. This is no big deal. Really. He was probably already running one for the task force."

"I should have thought of that. Explain there's nothing between us, so he'll call off the background. I just hope it's not too late." He scooped the eggs out of the pan and set their plates on the table, treating his command like any other friendly suggestion.

He was clearly worried something awful would

be revealed. But what? He couldn't be the county sheriff if he'd broken the law. That couldn't be a possibility. So what or who was he trying to protect?

"First off, do you really think I have that kind of control over the Commander? And second, I thought there was something between us. Am I wrong?"

"Go ahead and eat."

They both sat, coffee and breakfast growing cold while they sort of just stared at all of it. She didn't know what to do, almost afraid to say anything that might change his mind about telling her—whatever was horrible enough that he thought it would keep them apart. At least she assumed it would keep them apart. His seriousness seemed to indicate that, but it was hard to hypothesize correctly without any facts.

Silence was not her thing. She asked questions, got people to spill the beans all the time. Pete seemed to have mastered how to keep his mouth shut. How typical that she'd fallen hard and fast for someone who fit the strong-and-silent stereotype.

"Other than the professional reasons we shouldn't be involved, there's something very basic you should know," he finally said.

"Okay." That hurt. She really hadn't anticipated he'd say they shouldn't be involved. She better understood what biting your tongue meant. She literally bit the end of her tongue to keep her silence.

Neither of them lifted a fork. She was glued to the endless expressions crossing Pete's face. She might pass out from holding her breath waiting for him to talk.

"I can't leave Marfa."

"Is that all? I didn't expect you to. At least not now. If I do get the post outside the country, maybe you can visit. If you want to, that is. I mean, I'm not assuming anything because of what happened this morning." The words spilled out.

"I would if I could, but it's just not possible."

"Do you need a passport or are you afraid of flying?" He was so earnest and didn't seem as if he was going to explain the background comment. A million reasons popped into her head. Reasons she wanted to be true instead of the one thing that kept reverberating in the back of her mind.

"No and no." He shook his head and pushed his damp hair away from his face, clearly struggling with the decision to tell her.

She covered his hand, now on the table. "Whatever it is, you can trust me."

"Pete Morrison is not my real name."

"Honey told me about your adoption last week." She couldn't wait for his explanation and rushed forward, following the illogic of what he'd revealed. "So what is it? What secret are you protecting? I mean, you live here, everyone knows you. Those pictures back at the sheriff's office prove you grew up here. Your life looks like an open book."

"I'm not explaining this correctly."

He shoved back from the table and stared out the

window. "God, I don't know why I'm trying to explain this to you at all. I shouldn't. I wouldn't have brought it up if you hadn't warned me about the background check. I need you to call your father before it's too late, but I can't tell you why."

"Oh, no, you don't. You can't just drop that kind of…of request and not allow a question and answer." She stayed remarkably calm. She didn't know how, she just did. Much the same way she'd encouraged him this morning to face his attraction for her. She wanted him to trust her. Becoming all shrewish wouldn't accomplish that. "I didn't mean to rush you. I'm overly curious, if you couldn't tell that from knowing me a few days."

Waiting, she forced a bite of the bacon down without choking. Then a sip of cooling coffee.

"It's complicated," he said, dropping his chin to his chest.

"All the better to talk it through with a person who has an objective mind and can be unbiased." *Be patient.*

"I can't. I want to. It would be easier, but I can't." He walked around the kitchen, agitated.

Andrea placed her hands in her lap and watched without anxiously following him around the room. Part of the question on her mind was why Pete wanted her to know something he was clearly conflicted about revealing. Then again, why was she so excited that he'd begun to share with her?

"Whatever your real name, it won't change anything about our...friendship." If not a relationship, they could at least be friends.

"Not even if I'm the son of a murderer and never legally adopted by Joe?"

She swallowed hard after realizing her jaw had dropped open, totally unable to believe his statement. He was the son of a murderer and never adopted? It was more than a little hard to believe. "Those exact possibilities never crossed my mind."

"Believe me, I thought Joe was delusional from the heart attack when he told me what he'd done." The hurt he experienced was easy to see. His entire body slumped as he sat in the chair.

Andrea wanted to pull him into her arms and hold on as tight as he'd let her. She couldn't immediately call her dad. He'd want to know why, and if he hadn't begun the background check already, he would as soon as they hung up. "I hate to ask, Pete, but I'll need details to convince my father. Have you talked about this with Joe?"

"We've managed to avoid the conversation for six weeks."

"I don't think I could have waited. I'm too impatient and would want answers."

"Yeah, well. I didn't wait. My job does have some advantages. With a little research, I could put the facts together. I just don't know why my dad doesn't think it's a big deal. It could ruin everything he's worked for his entire life."

"You're talking about the illegal adoption? Maybe

there were extenuating circumstances. I'm sure he'd be forgiven."

Elbows on the table, Pete blocked showing his emotions to her by resting his head on his hands. There were very few times when she felt completely lost. This was one of them. Did he need comforting or someone to vent to?

He looked up, and his eyes sparkled with near tears. And she knew…no matter what he needed, she wanted to comfort him. She also knew exactly why it all mattered…she was falling in love with the whole man. Not just his dimples.

Chapter Twenty-One

Stupid. He'd blurted out his dad's well-kept secret. Just spilled his guts to a woman he hadn't known a week. The daughter of a man who could dig into his past and destroy everything he knew. And everything his father had sacrificed for his entire life.

"Are you okay, Pete?" Andrea asked.

Yeah, he was okay. He wanted to be angry at his dad. He was angry. Then he felt guilty. That had been the cycle for the past six weeks. How could he blame the man who'd raised him with no obligation to do so? It hurt…the betrayal. Pete hadn't realized how much.

"I'm not sure I can forgive him. He's lied to me for over twenty-five years. Upholding the law has been his entire life. He made it my entire life. And yet everything's been a lie."

"Not the way he feels about you." Her hand rubbed his shoulder, trying to comfort him. "Anyone who meets the two of you can tell how much he cares."

"I don't want to be the reason he loses everything. Can you call Commander Allen?"

"I don't think it's a good idea to bring the situation to his attention. Maybe he's not digging into your past at all. He hasn't removed you from the task force, which would happen if he'd discovered your identity doesn't exist. Where did Joe get your birth certificate? Things like that?"

"I don't have one. That's what started this whole mess. County Administration entered my interim-sheriff status into the system and notified me they didn't have a copy of my Social Security card or birth certificate. Dad admitted that he twisted some arms to get me hired back before the updated system was installed. He also said my Social Security number is a fake. He bought it before I started school, so I had no idea."

Andrea's jaw dropped again. Sort of the way his had done when he'd found out.

She quickly recovered. "That seems..."

"Very illegal, as in he's bound to do jail time." Thus his dilemma. Having a government agency dig into his past would expose his father no matter what good intentions he had long ago.

"No wonder you're worried for him. He must have had a good reason to go to such lengths."

"I wouldn't know. I haven't asked."

"You have to be the least curious man I've ever met." She left the table to microwave her breakfast. "Obviously, you're going to ask him, right? I mean, you need to hear the entire story. Want me to heat up your plate?"

No longer hungry, he shook his head. If he didn't know how smart Andrea Allen was, he'd wonder about her stream-of-consciousness conversation. All in all, he liked it. More often than he'd admit out loud, he silently chuckled at how her mind worked and made him stay on his toes.

Every time he turned around he was amazed by how casual and accepting she was of their situation. Telling her he was the son of a murderer stopped her as long as it took to hiccup. Then she was asking to warm his breakfast.

Damn, the woman made him want more. More of her. More of life. Just…more. Until he'd met her, it had never crossed his mind. Now that it was out of his reach, he ached for a chance.

She was back at the table, silently eating and occasionally looking at him. He could tell she was dying to ask more questions. He didn't know if he was ready to answer.

"Do I smell bacon?" his dad asked as soon as the front door opened.

"In here, Dad."

He barreled around the corner. "Good, you're still awake." He looked at the table, grabbed a slice of bacon from Pete's plate and nodded toward Andrea. "I can see by the look on his face that you asked him. About dang time. You tell her?" he asked his son.

Pete nodded, and Andrea sipped the last of her coffee. He wondered how long her silence would last before she'd shoot a list of questions for his father.

"Good," his dad continued, twirling the chair around to sit. "We need to get this out in the open, and you need to stop trying to protect me."

"Outside." Pete liked Andrea, but this was private. He needed the reason before he shared it with anyone—if he ever shared it.

"You don't want her to know why?"

"I was just telling Pete that I'm really tired. You guys talk. I'm plugging in my earphones, turning on some music." She lifted the tablet and forced a yawn. "I'll be out before you can say right ascension." The blank look on his dad's face must have encouraged her to explain. "It's an astronomer's term that... Sorry, never mind me. I'm heading to bed."

Andrea backed out of the room. Her bedroom door clicked shut softly, and he was alone with his dad. Biological or adopted, legal or not—Joe Morrison would always be his dad. He'd already forgiven him.

"I shouldn't be surprised at not being able to follow her talk too much. Andrea tried to tell me what she was looking at through the telescope the first time I picked her up. Couldn't make hide nor hair of it. She let me take a peek, though. It was almost as pretty as her." His dad poured himself a cup of coffee from the pot that rarely turned off.

"She's definitely a smart woman." Pete realized what he'd said and tried to ignore his dad's inquisitive raised eyebrow. "Yeah, you meant the picture in the telescope. I got it. But she is smart and gives good advice."

"Like…"

"Like how I should have asked you about my *adoption* as soon as you were out of the hospital. I can't believe that the man who preached at me about doing what was right my entire life had been breaking the law the entire time."

Joe leaned on the counter, just as Pete had earlier, talking to Andrea. He held his coffee cup the same way as his dad.

"The first four months you were here, I never had to ask for a babysitter when I went to work. The church organized it. You know, people say we look alike. It was easy for everyone to believe you were my grand-nephew. It was also easy for them to look the other way about certain things."

"Seriously, Dad, you risked everything. Why did you do it?"

"The why part is an easy answer. You. I did it for you."

"I need a little more than that, Dad."

"It was the right thing to do, son. And I'd do it again."

Joe sat at the table, taking Andrea's place. The tanned skin around his eyes crinkled with his smile. "When you said you knew who your father was, I'm assuming you figured it out after I said I arrested him."

"I figured it had to be someone outside Presidio County about the time I came to live with you. You only arrested three people. Two were transferred to San Antonio and one ended up in Huntsville State Prison. Philip Stanley sat on death row for eleven years. Just after my fourteenth birthday you took a trip to see him, didn't you? Did you go for the execution?"

"That's right." He sipped from the cup. "Sad day. He'd robbed a liquor store in El Paso. Shot and killed the attendant."

"The report said you talked him into releasing hostages at a house south of here."

"A family of four. They moved not too long after that. I think their five-year-old son made more of an impact on Phil than I did trying to get him to let them go. Something the kid did made him want you to grow up in a home and be happy. He loved you in his own way. He let the people go when I gave my word I'd find your maternal grandparents. His were already gone. I tried. Believe me. I verified straight off that your mother was deceased. It took nine months to discover that her parents had passed on before you were born."

"And I lived with you for that time? Why didn't you turn me over to foster care?"

"Gave my word I wouldn't. He was scared you'd turn out like him and made me promise no foster homes." He cleared his throat and leaned back in the chair. "I'd already told everyone you were my nephew. Hell, Sheriff Grimshaw is the one who encouraged me to give my word at the house. He's the one who helped me find information on your family."

"So Uncle Russ knew and even helped you."

"Yeah. He vouched for me and thought of you as part of his family, too. We convinced ourselves we were doing the right thing. Two old bachelors taking on a kid who we were determined would not end up like his old man. We thought about the foster program, but after you'd been here that long, they wouldn't have given you to me."

"How'd you enroll me in school? Didn't I need records?"

"We actually used his wife's Social Security number for school. It's not so hard to enroll as long as you had shot records. Everyone around here knew your story by then. No one pressed us. Russ got the county to hire you. I winked a couple of times to make people forget your paperwork was incomplete."

"You know you can go to jail."

"Son, no one cares. You're a good man. This won't make any difference in you being sheriff."

"Dad, Andrea's father made me a part of his task force. He's probably got people vetting me right now. That means a background check. They'll find the falsified information. Believe me, the government cares."

"I don't see why it should matter now. We can get everything straightened out, maybe legally change your name. You haven't done anything wrong."

"Dammit, Dad. Don't sit there and act like this isn't a game changer." He would have been yelling. If there wasn't a guest in the house, he probably would have been ranting a little at how nonchalantly his dad was accepting their secret was out.

Yes, it was their secret now. People would assume Pete had known about his adoption circumstances. As close as he was to Joe, no one would believe otherwise.

His dad seemed remarkably calm when he turned to him with no smile, just a gleam in his eyes. He looked free of a huge burden. "Son, I know the gravity of the situation. I'm accepting full responsibility. If the world finds out, then the world finds out."

"They don't have to find out. I can resign, stop Commander Allen from moving forward with the vetting process."

"No way. Absolutely not."

"Dad, what's impossible is to ignore this ticking time bomb. No ifs, ands or buts. It's going off. Only a question of when."

"I disagree. There's—"

"Excuse me." Andrea dashed into the room. One ear pod dangling, one still in position, tablet in hand, looking as bright as sunshine. "I know you two need to talk, but this… It just can't wait. I'm so sorry for interrupting. But can I? Interrupt, I mean?"

"Sure," his father said. "Have a seat."

Pete would have rather finished their conversation, devising a game plan. Whatever she'd found, Andrea seemed about to burst with excitement. She probably couldn't wait.

"Oh, I can't sit, thanks. This is… Well, you have to read it for yourself, but I think Sharon was working with those men. Or at least it seems that way to me. Do you want to call the rest of the task force? Maybe get their take on it?"

"You might want to show us what you're talking about first." Pete tried to slow her down.

"Oh, I was doing it again. My apologies." Standing between him and his father, she set the tablet on the table and swiped the screen. "An email popped up addressed to Sharon from an unknown sender."

She touched the screen a second time, bringing up the email program.

We'll pay $500 if you get her on her own. Let us know when and where. Don't cross us, Sharon. You know what kind of trouble you'll be in if things go wrong.

"So what do you think?" she asked.

"This could mean anything," he answered. "Are there more emails?"

"A couple. She sent the information about me

taking her place on Friday night at the Viewing Area, right down to the license tag on her car."

"Then you were set up."

"How did you find the emails?" his dad asked.

Andrea leaned on his shoulder. The movement was so casual he wasn't certain she knew she was there. Nice, yet very telling when his dad raised an eyebrow and the corner of his mouth in a half smile.

"This is a university-issued tablet. I've been utilizing it, inputting my data and notes. Those creeps stole my music last week, so I thought I'd listen from my cloud. I haven't been on the internet, since Dad asked me not to. But when I went to sign in, the device automatically logged in as Sharon. She must have been the last user and forgotten to log out." She shook his shoulders with her excitement.

Pete scrolled through some of the other messages. "Why wasn't this turned over to Commander Allen's team? They're better equipped to trace where the message came from. They collected her laptop and cell from the car fire—or at least what was left of it."

"I guess no one thought about the tablet. The University of Texas owns it and all the students use it."

"I'll drive the tablet over to Cord's place."

"Not so fast, please," Andrea said, trying unsuccessfully to snatch it from his grasp. They both held it inches above the tabletop.

The look on her face sort of shouted that she wanted to use the clue herself. "No way, Andrea.

We've got to get this to Cord's team. I'm not putting you in danger again."

"We should check with the DEA agent at the task force meeting. Maybe she knows how to trace the sender or who to contact about it."

Pete stood, grabbing her shoulders securely enough to get her attention. "We are not tracking down whoever sent this email."

"But they might have Sharon."

"I agree. But it's not my job." He'd guessed why she'd stayed at the observatory just after her father left. He'd come right out and accused them of using her to draw Logan's murderers into the open. But no one else had confirmed it. If they didn't give him a direct order, he could play along and focus on his assignment.

"You're kidding. Why are you on the task force, then?"

"To babysit."

His decision not to search for her friend wasn't the only contribution to her look of dissatisfaction. She was disappointed in him. And he could live with that. As long as it kept her safe.

Chapter Twenty-Two

Studying the chessboards along the edge of his study was comforting. It took his mind off other problems and somehow helped him eventually resolve those problems. Then his eyes landed on Patrice.

Once again, she sat on the edge of her chair, sipping her wine, ready for his instructions. She'd behaved well during their last encounter, following his instructions to the letter. As a result, she was conducting herself with cautious obedience.

The delivery was scheduled to take place in two days' time. The details were complete, with the exception of Andrea Allen in his possession. The risks were much higher without her as a pawn. He kept reworking the board, wanting a different outcome.

The only way to guarantee victory was his original plan. Throw another distraction into the laps of the Border Protection officers and they'd weaken. If they were searching for their commander's daughter, there would be fewer officers searching for his shipment.

Yes, his tactics might need to change, but the fundamental overall strategy was sound and needed to stay in play. Therefore, it was essential to capture his opponent's queen.

"Do you still have the college girl?"

Patrice looked up quickly, setting her wine on his glass table. "Yes, of course. You said to ship her south with the guns and let the men split the money when they sold her. Blondes bring a good price."

"Good. Good." He studied his third game board, anticipating a Steinitz strategy.

"There's one more thing, Mr. Rook. Our mutual friends would like you to oversee the transfer yourself."

"Certainly. Patrice, have I ever told you about Wilhelm Steinitz? He developed several rules of chess. The first states that the right to attack belongs to the person with the positional advantage. Since I am in the superior position of knowing what lies ahead, I believe I have an obligation to attack or lead. If I fail to attack, I deserve for the advantage to evaporate."

"I think I know what you're saying." Her look of utter confusion confirmed she did not.

"Steinitz thought the attack should always be made on your opponent's weakest square. Do you know what that is for the men trying to find us?"

She shook her head.

"Andrea Allen."

"She has around-the-clock protection. Do you have a plan to abduct her?"

"I do. And I'll need the university student. How soon can we have her available?"

"I can get her back by tomorrow. I'll need a drop-off point."

"Certainly." Ah, yes. If he moved his king's rook… "Hand me my phone."

She complied, and he texted the new position of his rook. If his opponent's moves were as predictable as he projected, in two moves he would run the board.

"Based on Miss Allen's personality and the inexperience of the new sheriff, I think our problem will be resolved soon. Let's drop her roommate near the abandoned southwest camp."

"And what then?"

"I'll provide you instructions. Do you need more wine?" She shook her head, and he locked the door. "After a very long week, I'm in the mood for a bit of fun."

There was a moment—just a slight raise of her delicate eyebrow—where Patrice had a look of calculated control. He didn't care to think about it twice. She unzipped her leather skirt and let it fall over her slim hips. She could make the arrangements for the girl's transportation soon.

The thought of Andrea Allen sitting in Patrice's place excited him to his core. Extracting his pleasure shouldn't take long at all.

Chapter Twenty-Three

Father and son had both picked her up from the observatory this morning. They held a conversation in the front seat while Andrea stared out the window at the same rocks as yesterday and the day before and the day before that. Boring terrain? She wouldn't admit to anyone that she secretly loved it. Watching the sun rise here was different from anyplace she'd ever lived, and the stars… The stars were amazing. She could look at them every night for a lifetime.

"Not a word since I told her no yesterday," Pete answered Joe.

Joe had offered the front passenger seat to her, but she'd moved past him and climbed into the back. Alone, free from distractions. Without staring at Pete, she could search the sunrise for answers to all the confusing questions she'd been left with yesterday.

Search, but not find. She was still as confused as ever. Needing to be involved in finding Sharon.

Scared that she might be allowed to participate. Frightened that she wouldn't. Ultimate confusion.

She forced herself to count the different varieties of trees instead of sneaking a peek at Pete. The conversation with his dad was obviously meant to pique her curiosity. Both men were blatantly attempting to get her to jump in and talk to them. She'd easily ignored them both yesterday afternoon, closed off in her bedroom sanctuary. Today would definitely be harder.

Especially when she wanted to ask if the task force had discovered anything from the tablet Sharon had used. Nope, she wasn't going to talk to him. She might ask Joe later, but he was helping Pete annoy her at the moment.

"I'm just doing my job. You'd think she'd understand how a protection detail works," Joe said. "Someone protects the gal needing protecting. The rest of the task force runs down the information about secretive emails implicating a missing student."

"Secret?" she began, then stopped herself. No talking. Pete had insulted her and hadn't bothered to apologize. Point in fact, when she'd taken her dinner to her room he'd shouted after she was around the corner that he wouldn't apologize for thinking of her safety first.

It was killing her not to ask a gazillion questions. Where was Sharon? Why hadn't Joe just legally adopted Pete? What made him lie all these years?

But more important, how did Pete feel about his father's explanation?

It appeared that whatever the explanation, Pete had accepted it and moved on. His relationship with his dad seemed as strong as ever. Another reason she wanted to talk was that she had her own news to share. Each morning, she'd enjoyed filling Joe in on her project, even if he rarely understood what she said. It felt good to talk about the progress and the setbacks. Darn it. And last night had been one setback after another.

Pete made the final turn onto the last road to their house when the county radio squeaked. "Pete, you there?"

"Yeah, Honey. What do you need?"

"We've got a call here for Miss Allen. She still with you? Want us to patch it through?"

"Who's calling?"

"A woman just keeps saying it's an emergency and asks for a number to reach her. I'd assume it's no one from her work, since she was there all night. Her parents have your number, right?"

"Patch it through and run a trace." Pete passed the microphone to her. "This doesn't seem right, Andrea. You will not give them a number to call you directly. Not until we establish who it really is. Got it?"

"Yes."

He pulled next to the barn when the radio crackled again. "Andrea?"

"Sharon? Thank God, you're alive. Where are you? What happened?"

Pete covered her hand and lifted her thumb from the microphone. "Let her talk, Andrea. We need some details."

"They won't let me go unless you bring…" Sharon whimpered. "I'm sorry, I don't understand."

Andrea was frozen with fear. She couldn't press the button to ask if Sharon was still connected. She could hardly breathe, wondering what demands these vultures were going to make. And she was scared to death she wouldn't be able to help.

All the questions from earlier dissipated into the ozone. They seemed petty in comparison to someone's life.

"Sharon? Are you there?" Andrea jumped when she heard a short scream, then crying. "Sharon!"

"Three thousand dollars. They want money…you and only you…" Sharon continued to cry. "Bring it at sunset tonight. The…coordinates… Oh, God, are you ready to write this down?"

Joe wrote the numbers on Pete's notepad he'd removed from the glove box.

"Do you know where you are?" Andrea asked, her eyes locking with Pete's.

"No." More crying. "Andrea, please come. I'll pay you back, I swear." Sharon's sobbing was followed by another short scream as if she'd been struck.

"Whoever you are, the money's not a problem. Don't hurt her!"

"I'm scared." The static from the call stopped.

"We'll find you." She'd moved closer to the front seat and didn't realize that she was clinging to Pete's hand. "Do you think she heard me?"

"Yes," Joe said, patting her shoulder.

She kept her eyes on Pete. His lips flattened, and he nodded ever so slightly. He didn't like it. "Those coordinates sound like the box canyon on Nick Burke's place where they had the shoot-out with the McCreas."

"I was thinking the same thing," Joe said. "That means we need horses, and they don't actually expect her to be alone. I'll get in touch with Burke. I assume you're heading to talk to Cord. You taking Andrea?"

"Of course he is," she said to both men, who continued to ignore her.

"She's got to go somewhere. She won't be safe here alone."

"You know it's an ambush." Joe nodded, reaffirming his statement.

"I think they've had a reason for everything they've done." Pete kept hold of her hand. "This fits in with Cord's informant hearing something would be going down during the UFO Border Zone conference." He looked at her. "I meant to tell you about the potential threat yesterday, but we sort of changed the subject."

She liked the feel of his strong fingers wrapped around hers. She could get used to that feeling, the sense of having someone there for you. Even if he was carefully controlling his emotions and hiding behind circumstances.

"Son of a—" Joe mumbled. "That's a couple of thousand extra faces to sort through. Half of 'em will be in alien costumes."

"Does anyone care what I think?" Andrea asked. Father and son stared at each other instead of laughing outright. They were the ones with experience. She knew that.

Fortunately, their silent laughter was interrupted by another squawk of the radio. "We couldn't get a trace, Pete. You want me to bring the deputies in to help? What kind of support do you need?"

"Keep them in Presidio with the want-to-be aliens until McCrea orders otherwise." He set the microphone down and rubbed his chin.

"Why ransom the girl back today?" Joe asked.

Pete snapped his fingers. "Another distraction. The UFO Border Zone starts this afternoon. It's the perfect time to smuggle guns with all those aliens running around all night."

"Night of aliens?" The phrase popped into her mind and she knew exactly where she'd first heard it. "The undercover man in the desert said 'night of aliens' before he passed out. The camera was in the back with him."

"Maybe he tried to warn you or give you the group's location. Maybe he knew more and left the info on the camera after the accident. There was no way to know when he actually died, especially when they stole his body."

"If he did say something else, I don't remember. The recording would be on that missing camera. Didn't anyone look for it after the meeting?" She sat on the edge of the seat, then fell backward as realization dawned. "Oh, my gosh, whoever has Sharon must not have the camera or they'd know what was recorded, right? That's why they need me. To see if I know the plans. Do you think the agent could have hidden the camera and it's still in the car?"

"It's possible," Joe said. "We weren't looking for a camera at the crime scene."

"I'll have Hardy go over and take another look. Maybe he'll get lucky and we can get you out of this mess."

"You know it doesn't matter if he finds it." Andrea knew this was the reason she'd agreed to stay. "We don't have any choice. We still have to go or they'll know we've figured out their plans. Sharon will be at those coordinates and we need to save her. That's all that matters. Three men have died already. Sharon has her whole life in front of her."

"So do you," Pete stated simply. "You aren't going."

"I know, I know. Your job is to babysit me." She dropped the warmth of his hand, scooted across the seat and opened her door before looking his direction. "Look for the camera. I hope the information we need is on it. But I'm still going. You can't stop me."

"Is that a challenge?"

She wouldn't argue now. She knew how to defend a position and had even taken classes on the subject. Her dad's instructions were clear. She just needed to prepare her plan of attack.

"JUST WANTED TO say again how much I appreciate you coming here to the ranch, Cord." Pete was relieved he hadn't needed to demand the task force come to them. "I don't want to move Andrea yet."

"It made sense. Half of us were already here," Agent Conrad said, then shrugged.

Andrea smiled at him, suggesting her position on the task force had been confirmed.

"Miss Allen is not a member of this team," he corrected, and no one challenged him. "Did you discover anything about the emails?"

He moved behind Andrea, keeping his hands on the back of her chair instead of reaching out to touch the back of her neck. If he looked at her, someone might overanalyze how long he stared or why he felt such a strong urge to shout that she needed to be flown out of the area immediately.

"Mind you, I'm only working with this one account, but I don't think she meant Andrea any harm. At least it doesn't seem so. If I took a guess, I think the person making the suggestions to her is a female."

"How can you get that?" Cord asked.

"The sentence structure and choice of words. I've had a little profiling. In an earlier email, the sender states they're friends with you, Andrea."

Everyone looked first at Andrea and then toward him, standing directly behind her. Everyone, with the exception of his dad, who just shook his head and sighed.

"That's ridiculous. I don't know anyone around here and even if I did, does it really make sense to want to meet me in the middle of nowhere? I would never have agreed to that." Andrea tried to stand up.

Pete placed his hand on her shoulder, keeping her in the chair. They hadn't really spoken since the day before, but it didn't seem to matter. She immediately responded with a deep breath and seemed a little less tense. By Cord's compressed lips, he hadn't missed the gesture.

Agent Conrad sat on her hands. Her gaze dropped to her lap. She was busting buttons to keep herself from responding.

"I think Beth is implying that someone told Sharon they were trying to surprise you and not to ask you about it. And no one here thinks she did," his dad said to Andrea with complete calm.

Absolutely the calmest man he knew, Joe stretched back in his favorite chair, hands behind his neck, ankles crossed under the coffee table. He didn't seem worried that a woman's life was in danger. The others in the room might misinterpret his calmness for not caring, but Pete knew different.

In that moment, the clarity of how his father had been over twenty-five years ago smacked into Pete. Calm and rational. Two things his father had always been. He would have been no different confronting a murderer and promising that man his son wouldn't face the same fate.

He would have meant every word. And then kept his word. And he had. The price just might be the expense of his entire career.

There was nothing Pete could do at the moment to help his dad. He caught his hands slipping toward Andrea's shoulders and pulled them away, tucking them into his pockets before taking a step back. He glanced around the room. Only Cord had a disapproving frown on his face.

Andrea popped up and went to the window. "I just need to get to a bank to withdraw the three thousand dollars."

"Why that amount?" Agent Conrad asked. "Does it strike anyone else as an odd amount for a ransom? I mean, it's not an overly large sum. Many would have that in their bank account."

"It's not a problem for me to pay."

"Why do you think it's a low amount?" Cord rose and guided Andrea away from the windows.

Her long sigh assured everyone in the room just how tired she was of being kept safe. Pete knew she was ready for the forced protective custody to be over. "Shouldn't we get started? It takes forever to get from place to place around here."

Cord swiped a hand over the bottom half of his face. "Nick's bringing extra horses and will help with the tracking—if necessary. We're leaving from here, Andrea."

"When? I need to change and then get to the bank."

"Cord brought the ransom. You're not going," Pete stated, again waiting for someone to tell him different. He knew the bomb would be dropped. Just not by whom.

"What do you mean?" Andrea marched toward him, sticking her hands on her hips, ready to do battle. "Of course I'm going. I have to go. They won't release Sharon if I don't."

"No. Agent Conrad's going in your place." He could try. They all knew why she'd stayed in Marfa even if no one said it out loud. She was the bait. But he could try to keep her out of the frying pan.

"Um, Pete," Cord interrupted.

At the same time, Beth Conrad shook her head. "I'm not sure that's wise."

Pete had made a decision. He no longer cared about being politically correct or following orders or whose orders needed to be considered. "My job is to make sure this woman stays safe. That's not going to happen taking her into a trap. We all know it's a trap. The responsible thing is to have her stay with my dad."

He wanted to be the one to stay with her, protect her, make love to her again. But safe with his dad and a couple of trusted ranch hands would have to do.

"The responsibility isn't yours," Andrea stated firmly. "You know what my father already decided."

"I don't know how to ride a horse," Beth Conrad mumbled behind him.

"She'll be safer with us," Cord said, clapping a hand on his shoulder. "We can't do this without her."

He shrugged out from under the hand of the official leader of the task force. "This is a joke. Plain and simple. What you really mean to say is that Andrea's father has already decided she should go. Does he have a death wish for his daughter?"

A red haze seemed to tint the entire front room. Pete's blood pumped loudly through his veins while he concentrated on relaxing the tightness in his chest. Nick's truck and trailer turned onto the driveway. They'd be leaving soon. All of them.

Overruled again. At least he'd made his objections well-known.

"Nothing good's gonna come from this. Nothing." He slammed out the screen door, taking a deep breath, surprised at how betrayed he felt. "Acting sheriff or actual sheriff. Makes no difference when no one listens to a word you say."

Chapter Twenty-Four

They were on their way to rescue Sharon and had officially crossed over onto the Burke family ranch. Andrea had won and was with the rescue party. It was obvious to her that every person around her disagreed with the decision. No argument needed. Her father had left instructions that if the opportunity presented itself, she'd take an active role and try to lead them to the murderers.

So here she sat, sure to be saddle sore tomorrow even though the riding wasn't that difficult. Pete, Cord and the DEA agent—maybe even Joe—all considered her the weakest link. She knew that. The new guy who'd brought the extra horses, Nick, had raised a ruckus about bringing either woman.

None of them would allow her to carry a weapon. Ironically, her father had probably had a gun in her hands earlier than any of them. Well, maybe with the exception of Pete since Joe didn't have a wife telling him not to teach his son anything and everything.

The DEA agent tugged at the reins again, upsetting the beautiful sorrel she rode. Beth would be lucky if the mare didn't buck her off just to escape the woman's obvious inexperience. Then where would Sharon's rescue be?

"Loosen your grip and she'll follow the trail just fine," Nick Burke said to Agent Conrad.

"You're kidding me, right?" the agent replied, jerking the reins to the side. They continued arguing, exchanging little digs back and forth. Some under their breath, but mostly not.

"This will never work." Andrea was furious but kept her voice low enough for just Pete to hear her. "Agent Conrad might be the same height, but stuffing her hair into a hat won't fool anyone that she's me. She doesn't even know how to sit a horse. It's obvious to everyone she's petrified of the animal. It's old, as slow as Christmas, and she's still having trouble controlling it."

"We'll get there in time." Pete stayed calm and relaxed in the saddle.

In the week she'd known him, anxiety rarely showed through his controlled exterior. Stressful situations seemed to make him even more laid-back. He watched, waited.

And she was just the opposite. The more frustrated or excited she became, the more questions she asked. And at the moment she was very anxious for Sharon's benefit.

"What if they're watching us right now? I mean, anyone can tell she's not me."

He took a long look at Andrea's outfit. She knew exactly what he was thinking. They'd gone to great lengths to make her look like a guy, even setting her on a smaller, shorter horse so she'd look larger. The oversize Western hat on her head stayed in place with a leather tie.

"They don't know you're the one who can ride a horse. We're not certain they know about Agent Conrad being here at all. Keep your eyes open."

Beth Conrad's horse whinnied loudly and began dancing in circles. They'd never make it to the rendezvous point at this rate. Pete brought his horse closer. It was the first time since their task force meeting that the frown on his face had relaxed.

"Andrea, we won't be able to stop them from taking you. Do you know that?" The concern on his face broke her heart.

It should have frightened her.

"Cord informed Dad's team. They're tracking me. It'll be okay." As hard as it was to say the words, it was harder to believe them while she looked at the worry on Pete's face. He hadn't smiled all day and probably shouldn't, but she missed it. Missed the man who had teased her to nervous, unending babble.

Pete leaned in close, tugging her even closer. If anyone had fallen for her outfit before, her cover was totally blown when his lips devoured hers.

Excitement returned even with the cautioning clearing of Cord's throat.

"I know you think you have to go through with this, but you don't." Pete let his horse put a couple of feet between them.

"He's right," Cord added. "Say the word and we're heading back at a full gallop. There's no guarantee that Sharon will be released."

"But there's a chance."

Nick tried to help Beth by jumping off his horse and soothing the older mare.

"Very slim," Pete said.

"I have to do this. And we all know the real objective is to find their camp and the men responsible. We'll put a stop to the murders and find Sharon."

Pete exchanged a glance with Cord, making her feel naive. Well, maybe she was, but she had to try catching the person responsible for Logan's death.

"Remember what we said. Try to keep an idea of where you are. Landmarks, if you cross water, sounds like a train or lots of people." Pete rubbed her back. "If I can't stop you, just remember that I *will* find you. Got that?"

"Yes."

"Don't be a hero, Andrea. Just do what they say. Please," Pete whispered.

"If things don't go according to plan, just listen to us and do what we say. Okay?" Cord added. "You ready, Nick?"

Before Nick could respond, Beth exploded with

confidence behind them. "I can do this!" But a loud crack sounding like a single gunshot echoed through the mountains, giving their horses a different opinion. While the rest of them regained control, Beth's old mare bolted into the open area toward the wider end of the ravine.

"Dammit, she's lost control of the reins," Cord said, rising straighter in his saddle as if he could see more than a runaway horse carrying away their bait.

"I'll get her," Nick exclaimed, taking off before anyone could object. "Don't wait for us."

"You want to wait here?" Pete asked. "Or do we turn around and forget this farce?"

"We can't." Andrea could only think of her mission. The shadows were growing long behind them as the sun sank lower on the other side of the mountains. "We have to keep going for Sharon."

She shoved the hat off her head, letting the leather string dig a little into her throat as the wind caught it like a sail behind her. She tussled her short hair around, fluffing it a bit to let anyone watching know it was her. Pete was still close so she leaned and kissed him with all the passion she could. He kissed her back and looked stunned when she sat in her saddle again.

"We have to find Sharon." She kicked her horse and took the lead, trotting up the trail they'd been following.

"Andrea! Wait!" Pete shouted. "What are you doing?"

Both men called for her to stop. She would, just as

soon as she got over the next rise and it was too late to follow the DEA agent whose horse was still galloping in the opposite direction. She clicked to her own mare, kicking her sides just a little to get her to break the trotting motion. The path was smooth and level enough for a short, steady lope.

She topped the rise, slowing and coming face-to-face with six armed men. Horses and ATVs and gun barrels. No Sharon in sight. Her escort was several seconds behind her.

It was the trap Pete had anticipated. She'd been so determined—or stubborn—to save the young college student that she'd disregarded all the men's warnings. Midway in turning her horse around to get back to safety, a man leaped out and grabbed her waist. They fell to the ground and rolled, lucky four hooves didn't trample them. She kicked out, threw an elbow in the soft spot under his rib cage, but he held tight.

Nothing deterred him. They ended up with him on the ground, her on top of him. He slapped a dirty hand over her mouth tightly so she couldn't shout out and warn the men. She kept throwing punches until another man put his boot on her stomach and pointed his gun at her head.

"That's far enough," the man holding the gun said. "Throw your weapons to the ground. We don't want any death today."

At first, Andrea thought he was talking to her.

Then she realized that Pete and Cord had topped the hill.

"Let her go," Pete shouted.

"We have your money. Where's the girl?" Cord's weapon was still holstered.

Pete moved, his eyes searching hers. They both knew that these men weren't there for a hostage exchange. They were there to abduct the daughter of the man in charge of border patrol.

The man holding Andrea released her to two others, who quickly yanked her to her feet and zip-tied her wrists behind her. Pete began to swing his leg over the back of his horse to dismount, but the man with the gun shoved it in her back, tsking.

Pete cursed and kept his seat.

"I'll be okay." She answered his unasked question. Her father would certainly be tracking her, but she could see the determination in Pete's eyes that he'd find her no matter what the cost. She knew he'd keep his promise.

Countless times she told herself to expect this scenario, yet it was still frightening. They wanted her alive, otherwise they would have shot them all earlier. Why was the million-dollar question that her father and the DHS needed answered.

The men half lifted, half dragged her to an empty ATV.

"Wait. Isn't there some deal we can make?" Pete asked.

"Don't you want your money?" Cord shouted.

"You keep your pittance. The women are worth a lot more to me. We'll get more for not taking your money." The one pointing the gun laughed at their attempt. He straddled the ATV in front of her. "You can get off your horses now."

Two other men on horseback pointed their guns at Cord and Pete, waiting for them to follow instructions. The weapons they'd dropped earlier had already been picked up. They bent low against their own horses, grabbing the lawmen's fallen reins and leading them away.

As the horses passed Pete, he lunged, catching one of the men off guard and pulling him to the ground. The big man giving the orders held up his hand to stop his men. All stayed where they were while the one closest to Cord put a gun to his head. He froze while the fight continued.

The man Pete fought was young and seemed inexperienced. Pete got two or three punches in for every one he took. A final uppercut to the younger man's jaw had him out cold against the rocky trail.

Pete took a deep breath and wiped a little blood away from a split lip. A pistol was quickly pointed at the back of his neck, keeping him from moving.

"That was quite a show. The fight was good experience for my man and seemed only fair since he helped kill one of yours." He gestured for one of the ATV riders to drag the unconscious man to his vehicle. "Useless to make a move. There are many of us. Too many to fight, I think."

"No harm in trying." Pete spit blood toward the man who had murdered Logan.

"I think Jimmy would disagree with you."

"I will find you," Pete growled with confidence but kicked rocks with his feet. The leader laughed.

It could have been encouragement for her or a threat to the man calling the shots. She didn't know. His words gave her hope and she'd hang on to them as long as possible.

Both ATVs were started.

"If it were up to me, *amigos*, you'd never walk out of here. Not up to me today. Maybe next time. *Si?*" He saluted Cord and Pete and put the ATV in gear with a jerk. "Take their phones."

Pete and Cord had brought hand radios, which the armed men tossed to the ground and smashed. She looked at Pete as long as she could. She knew he was yelling, but she couldn't hear his words over the ATV engines. Hoping above all else that this would end quickly and positively, she tried to get her bearings.

Then they were bouncing over rough terrain and all she could think about was hanging on for dear life. She barely had a grip on the edge of the seat with her hands tied. One good bump and she could be dead against the rocks.

They were on the north side of a state highway. So she doubted they'd be riding horses and ATVs all the way to the border. So where would they take her? They hadn't scanned her for tracking devices and she could only pray they wouldn't before they arrived at their destination.

And if they did?

Would she vanish like Sharon?

Chapter Twenty-Five

"They lost one of the signals twenty minutes in. Just lost the second." Cord hung up the cell.

"Where? Where's the last place they had her?" The look on the Ranger's face told him he'd been instructed not to disclose that information. "Dammit, Cord. Tell me. You knew this was going to happen. We all did and we let her go through with it anyway. Stupid. I should have stopped her."

"Take a minute. You tried to talk her out of it."

"I didn't try hard enough."

"We're to wait here. Burke and Beth Conrad are still missing." Cord calmly pocketed the cell they'd picked up from his truck.

"Do you think they're dead? We didn't hear any shots. And if they'd wanted more hostages, why didn't they take us?"

"Too much trouble, I imagine. Same as killing us would have brought too many law enforcement agencies in here to muck up their plans. We sit tight and wait."

"No. Whatever's happening is going down in Presidio. That's what your informant said. You going to sit in the corner and accept your punishment or are you coming with me?"

"Now, hold on just one damn minute. We aren't being punished. We're part of a team." Cord defended the task force.

At the moment, the only loyalty Pete felt was to Andrea. He'd promised her. He wouldn't sit around and let that promise be broken by following orders. He'd already broken a couple.

"Well, this player's tired of sitting on the bench." He threw out the challenge, wanting the backup but willing to go alone. "You coming?"

Cord hesitated long enough to blink. "Yeah, I need my shotgun."

"Dispatch," Pete said into the microphone while he was waiting.

"Whatcha need, Pete?"

"Anyone heard from Hardy? I sent him on an errand and thought to hear back by now."

"I'll ask him. Be right back."

And what if they were monitoring the police bands? "Peach, have him call my dad at the house."

"You got it, Sheriff."

Pete pulled out the tracking device he'd borrowed from the county. He'd been using it with Andrea since dropping her off the first day at the observatory. "Good, it's still working."

"You can't be tracking Andrea."

"Nope. Do you think I risked getting shot in a fight I knew I couldn't win? I planted a tracker on that guy, Jimmy."

"You could have told us."

"What's the fun in that?" He switched the box on and watched for a light. Nothing. "If I had told anyone, Andrea would probably have found out. I didn't want her to give it away. I also wasn't certain you guys would approve. We need to get closer for it to pick up the signal."

"Or they found it and got rid of it just like Andrea's. The fight was risky." Cord shook his head in disbelief.

"But worth it since my tracker still has a chance. Let's going."

It would be the fastest he'd ever driven the sixty miles from Marfa to Presidio. Also one of the blackest nights until the full moon came up. He passed one other car, his flashing lights lit the fields on either side. They were taking a risk. Mainly him. Not with just the speed of the Tahoe...

"What if they took her somewhere else? I should have stayed in the mountains and tried to track them."

"Don't second-guess your decisions, Pete. You took a big risk dropping the pocketknife during the fight, then kicking rocks on top of it. If you hadn't, we might still be waiting on Nick and Agent Conrad to untie us."

"I was lucky they didn't just shoot me."

"If they'd planned to shoot us, they would have as soon as we got within range." Cord glanced at his cell again. "Still no word from Nick."

"He knows those mountains as good as either of us. The DEA agent's horse looked pretty spooked. Probably took him a while to catch up." Pete couldn't put much thought into Nick's problems. Every thought came back to getting to Presidio fast. A plan wouldn't hurt, either. But he had nothing. "Do you think we should have stuck with tracking Andrea's abductors?"

"Forget it. You couldn't see a trail in the dark. They had horses and ATVs. Three each, three pairs or six different possibilities. Presidio is our best shot. We both know that."

It was worse than trying to find a needle in a haystack. At least you had the haystack right in front of you. This time they had a town and all the surrounding area. Miles of border and no way of knowing which way the illegal goods were crossing. Guns into Mexico or drugs into the States. There'd be mass confusion with too many law enforcement agencies trying to call the shots.

"What are we looking for when we get there?" He knew it was a long shot. "Other than Jimmy's jacket that I'm tracking?"

"Your guess is as good as mine," Cord finally admitted.

"I was afraid you'd say that."

ANDREA WAS STILL WET. The men who'd abducted her had been prepared for any electronics that she carried. By dumping her in a barrel of water the tracking earrings her father had sent would be useless. They'd held her under until she'd almost passed out.

Afterward, the six men had split up. Their leader drove them both to an awaiting helicopter. They didn't bother to blindfold her for the first part of the trip, so she could see all the terrain. They hadn't crossed the Rio Grande, so they were still on the U.S. side of the border. That, at least, was something in her favor. The nearest town to the east would have been Marfa, but they flew south.

The only city or town that direction was Presidio. Once they landed they'd covered her eyes with a sleeping mask. She could see nothing but her feet. And there hadn't been one clue about Sharon. Nothing had been mentioned.

Cord's informant had been right. The undercover agent had been right. And Pete had definitely been right. She, on the other hand, had been terribly wrong. There was little hope that Pete or her father would find her. But hope was all she had... and her wits.

What could these men gain from her being here? Especially tonight?

Alone in a small metal room, no bigger than a storage crate, she could hear the low bass of a speaker. It wasn't coming from the other side of the door as she'd first thought. It was behind her, through the wall. Vibrating. She must be close to the concert in Presidio.

Low lighting from a battery-operated lamp. Two chairs and a card table. It didn't feel like a normal room. The low ceiling was made of the same material. She was in a storage container. Driving from Austin to West Texas, she must have seen hundreds of these containers transported by train.

If she could only get word to Pete. She didn't know how much time had passed while sitting there. She'd counted every rusty plank of the container and knew how many rivets held it together. Her wrists were numb, still tucked behind her back in the folding chair. It made it impossible to rest her head.

The door opened and in marched an unusual man. Unusual because he was tall, well-dressed in a very expensive suit and had white-blond hair. His hair among all the darker Hispanics in the city would stand out. He smoothed it flat before clapping his hands.

"Come now, don't tell me that no one cut your hands free." A guy appeared with a knife.

Who claps their hands for the hired help? But that's how he acted...as if everyone around him was beneath him. So far beneath him he didn't give any direction to the men who'd abducted her, just facial expressions that shouted to everyone.

"Who are you?"

"You may call me Mr. Rook."

A comfy armchair was brought in for him to use. Then a glass of wine. Andrea would have settled for a sip of water. Her mouth was so dry she'd seriously thought about sucking some of the water out of her shirt. Then she remembered the dirty barrel they'd tossed her inside.

Mr. Rook sat and sipped his wine while one of the hired help cut her restraints. A sigh escaped from her as she massaged life back into her arms.

"There's no reason to think about trying to leave. My men surround this little box. No one will hear your screams because of the concert. And no one will trace you to our little town on the border since we got rid of anything on your person."

"I…" Her hoarse voice sounded ancient. "I wouldn't be so sure of that."

"Yes, you think your incompetent sheriff will find you like he promised? We've taken every precaution to make certain he doesn't. And this time tomorrow, you'll be secured in my home away from home so I can make a longer-lasting deal with your father."

"And where's that?"

"You'll find out when the time comes." He sipped his wine again and didn't look the least bit rushed.

The crate door opened and a beautiful blonde in

a tight-fitting leather skirt and jacket joined them. She slid a phone across the table without a word. Mr. Rook held it to his ear and locked eyes with Andrea. Her spine and body shivered. The polite captor had disappeared. Hate and disgust oozed from him.

"I have your daughter. Speak, Andrea." He didn't switch the speaker on. She could barely hear her father's voice asking if she was okay.

"Can you hear me, Dad? I'm fine after my short trip. You were right—"

The woman cut her off by pressing three fingers against the base of her throat, choking her. Andrea jerked away, finally knocking the woman's grasp loose. She missed Rook's instructions for her father while coughing and trying to get her breath back.

He placed the phone on the table. "Time to get started."

The woman left.

"Start what?" She searched the small opening, but the door quickly closed. She couldn't see a thing except the woman walking down the stairs immediately at the door. "What are you really doing?"

The man stood, slapping her left cheek. "Tie her up and store her in one of the containers."

Andrea averted her face and watched through the hair hiding her eyes. The blond man spoke well, wore the suit well. She remembered what Pete said how most criminals forgot the shoes. This man's shoes were old but expensive and well-kept. His nails were well manicured like a businessman's.

There would be no answers from Rook. Just like the man who had brought her here had no answers.

Two men in green alien heads blindfolded her, grabbed her arms and then hauled her out the door. They kept her tight between them, dragging her about fifty yards before throwing her into another dark container. Was it strange that they hadn't hurt her? At least not yet?

Once the door was bolted shut, it was blacker than the blindfold she'd removed. She was stuck unless Pete found her. Her father's hands were tied because of national security.

She had to have faith in Pete. She did.

The confidence that Pete would find her was the strangest thing she'd ever experienced. It was more than just attraction. She admired his kindness, his humbleness. She especially admired—maybe even envied—his relationship with his father and how he was determined not to ruin him.

The darkness didn't seem as dark. She was surrounded by wooden crates probably filled with guns heading to Mexico. Her father and his men would be watching for a truckload of drugs headed north. Not a cargo container filled with guns going south.

She climbed to the top of the stack to wait.

Pete would be there. She just hoped it was soon.

Chapter Twenty-Six

Pete and Cord followed the tracking blip to the outskirts of Presidio. If they could find the man he'd fought with in the mountains, they might find Andrea. They were close. He'd been stopped about half a block from them for a while.

"Our chances are slim to none this is going to work." Cord adjusted the shoulder strap holding his weapons and slipped into his jacket.

"Better than just aimlessly searching through a thousand people dressed as aliens."

Cord's phone rang. "It's Commander Allen." He answered, "McCrea...Yes, sir." He punched the speaker button.

"He's using her to guarantee safe passage for a shipment of drugs," the Commander said. "Wants to drive straight up Highway 67 through the Port of Entry. He knows most of your men are here and wants me to personally wave the truck through. He's a brazen son of a bitch, that's for sure. When he called, I could hear loud concert music. He may be holding her at the festival like you thought. Can you find my girl before his truck gets away from us?"

Music? The band was scheduled to begin in fifteen minutes. Did they just want them to *think* she was at the concert?

"We might have a chance, sir. Pete dropped a tracker in one of the men's pockets. It was risky but seems to be paying off. We're on his trail now."

"Good thinking, son. I'm less than seven minutes away via helicopter from the Port of Entry. Call when you find her. I want this crazy SOB alive to uncover the extent of his operation. He has to know that I can't let drugs through even to save my daughter. Out."

Cord stuck the phone back inside his jacket. Pete couldn't see his face, hidden in shadow from the brim of his hat. But that meant the Ranger couldn't see Pete's, either. If he could, it would be filled with worry and doubt.

It was up to him to save Andrea. The Commander had as much as said there was nothing he could do. He dropped his chin to his chest again to watch the green dot on his screen inch forward.

"He's on the move," Pete told his partner. They'd left the vehicle about half a block back. "He's heading for the festival. If he gets there, it'll be easier for him to disappear."

They turned and ran, this time with Cord driving while Pete watched the blip.

"Not if we have anything to do with it." Cord shoved his foot on the gas.

They both buckled up as they sped through the backstreets. They stopped midblock just ahead of whatever vehicle Jimmy—or his jacket—was in. An old pickup barreled down the street, skidding to a halt when its occupants spied the flashing lights.

Fortunately, it was late at night and Cord was a good driver. He spun the Tahoe, pushed the gas and missed the old vehicles on the side of the street. Within minutes they had Jimmy and his *compadre* in cuffs. Pointing the shotgun out the window at the driver helped.

"Hands flat on the dashboard, you murdering son of a bitch," Pete yelled from the window as he covered Cord heading toward the truck.

Both men complied. Jimmy was in the driver's seat. When he recognized Pete, his head dropped backward in defeat. Then he began chattering in Spanish to his passenger, who Pete recognized as one of the other horsemen at Andrea's abduction.

It didn't take long to get Jimmy's story. Hired help for a few days. The guy who had hired him for the trip to the mountains said to meet him at the festival. Everyone helping tonight was to wear an alien mask that covered their entire head. Those were the only instructions. Just show up.

Pete looked inside Jimmy's truck, picking up an alien mask. *Why the mask? Who does he need to hide from?* "Distractions."

"What?" Cord looked up from settling the second prisoner into the backseat. The Tahoe had been equipped with handles to handcuff passengers into place.

"Everything this head honcho has done so far has been about distractions. So why tell the head of Border Security that you're bringing a shipment into the States? Why abduct his daughter and threaten him when you could continue to sneak under the radar?" Pete looked at the crate in the pickup bed.

"If it's a distraction, then what's he really up to?" Cord asked, not dismissing Pete's theory. "Probable cause applies if we open a sealed crate."

Pete retrieved the tire iron from the Tahoe and jumped into the back of the truck. "We up the security coming into the country and don't concentrate on what's going out." He pried the top off the crate, then lifted a .38 Special to show Cord. "Second possibility is that he's ferrying guns south just like usual. There's a variety of handguns here. Not packed well. Probably straw purchases."

Cord slapped the hood of the Tahoe. "It's so simple it has to be right. That's why his men are meeting on this side of the border. Allen should be able to get some air support, but I don't know how quick. I'm guessing that you're going to search for Andrea."

"It's my job, my primary assignment."

"And the right thing to do." Cord clapped his shoulder as he walked around the front of the service vehicle. "I'll call Allen with the update. We shouldn't split up, but I don't see that we have a choice."

"I'll pose as Jimmy, find out what's going down and where if I can. But I will find Andrea." Pete dropped his hat onto the front seat for safekeeping. It wouldn't fit on top of the alien mask he intended to wear when he found Andrea. "Keep your head down, man."

"You, too, and good luck," Cord called out as he got in the Tahoe. He'd take Jimmy and his partner with him to the border crossing. He'd meet up with Commander Allen to see if either man had more information about their unnamed opponent or his plans.

Saving Andrea was Pete's duty, but much more than that. He'd promised to find her and he meant to keep his promise. The first step was to infiltrate wherever they were gathering.

He drove Jimmy's truck to the outskirts of the festival. The concert was in full swing. If there were any people attending not in costume, he couldn't see them. But since both the men they'd arrested were supposed to wear identical masks, he'd look for more of the same. Jimmy was slightly larger around than Pete, but the extra fabric of his denim jacket covered the pistol at the small of Pete's back. He was ready to pull the mask over his head when his cell rang.

"Pete, I found it," Hardy yelled excitedly. "The

camera was hooked under the seat and stuck clear up at the top of the metal springs. I guess it got wrapped there during the crash. There's a recording with a picture before the car rolls. Shoot, that dude was messed up bad. Then there's only sound... Man oh man, the guy you found had a lot to say about a drug operation and a Mr. Rook who runs the whole dang thing. He lives in Mexico, but he's supposed to be there in Presidio tonight. You want me to bring it to you?"

"Hardy, slow down. Lock the camera in evidence. Did he say where they're meeting?"

"Something about masked men and a stage. Oh, and the password is...I have it here in my notes. I wrote it down. There, king's rook checkmate."

"Thanks, Hardy. You've done a great job. Secure the camera and you can get back to patrol now."

"Yes, sir."

Pete stowed his phone in the truck along with his identification and county-issued shirt. His white tee fit in with the crowd better and he couldn't risk being spotted as the sheriff. He pulled the mask over his head and drove the perimeter of the parking lot, searching for more green aliens.

The plastic mask was hot, hard to breathe through and limited his line of sight. But it did its job protecting his identity. He passed right by two of his deputies without a second glance. The variety of costumes—some elaborate and some just face paint—were impressive. The people impersonating aliens posed for pictures with those who weren't. Some took it seriously, beeping a make-believe language in the background.

On the edge of the crowd, an identical alien spun full circle. Trying to find something or someone? Pete hung back, waiting for the fellow to lead the way.

A couple of minutes later he was following four or five little green men and a woman. These were most likely ordinary people purchasing guns with cartel money. The smaller crates they carried weren't disguised. No bogus labeling. Different sizes and styles. Most weren't crates at all, just plastic tubs. He stayed at the back of the group. No one asked him for a password. No one acted like he was there at all.

At the back of the stage were half a dozen men all in the same masks, loading wooden crates, boxes or tubs like what was in the back of Jimmy's truck into a twenty-foot steel shipping container. Mask or no mask, he recognized the big guy from the ATV earlier. He was wearing the same clothes and carrying the same shotgun.

Where was Andrea?

The boxes brought in were stored in wooden crates that were then loaded inside the steel containers on the big rigs. But where were the trucks going? No one would be stupid enough to drive across the border so openly. Of course, he wouldn't think that the cartel would so openly gather the guns they were going to smuggle at a concert where county deputies and Presidio cops were stationed.

"Hey, you," the big guy said in his direction. "Where's your shipment? Get it loaded in the second rig."

Pete acknowledged him with a nod and ran back to Jimmy's truck. He had to send a message to McCrea. He dialed, and another alien tapped on the window, and a guy pulled off his mask to talk.

"Hey, man. You need help carrying— You ain't Jimmy."

Pete dropped the cell on the seat and shoved the door open, knocking the alien back a step. "Sorry, man. Jimmy said I could charge my phone."

"You're lying. No way Jimmy lets you in his truck." The guy's alien mask dropped to the ground.

"No, really. I don't want trouble."

The man punched him hard in the stomach, stealing Pete's breath for a second. He straightened, fighting the pain. "You got this all wrong."

Pete didn't want any attention. If law enforcement broke up the fight, his deputies would recognize him. Then the smugglers would know. He'd never find Andrea.

Pete allowed Jimmy's friend to grab his collar and drag him back to the light of the truck cab. He reached for his gun when the man saw the badge on his shirt. Before the guy could open his mouth, Pete had the barrel shoved under his chin.

"Not a damn word. Where do they have the girl?"

His prisoner shook his head and shrugged. Which was probably the truth. The likelihood that she was here was slim to none. What was he going to do with him? He cuffed the guy's hands behind his back and shoved him to the pickup seat. "Now what?"

"Now you're a dead man. That's what."

"Pete? Did you find something?" McCrea had answered and was still on the phone.

Pete clicked the speaker button and shoved the tail of his shirt into his prisoner's mouth. "Yeah, they're smuggling guns across the border on big rigs. Don't know the route yet. Send men behind the concert stage and locate Jimmy's truck in the lot. Out." He tied the sleeves behind the man's head, effectively gagging him before he shoved the door shut and dropped the cell in the jacket pocket, then grabbed the guns.

This area would be swarming with law enforcement, alerting the smugglers to the bust. He had to find Andrea's location in the next few minutes or it would be hopeless. Disguised and carrying the tub of handguns, he fell into a short line and set it inside the shipping container. It was easy to get a good look inside in spite of the late hour because of the concert lights. But there was nothing but boxes of guns or ammo. Four steel containers and very few people in masks left around. He sneaked around to the opposite side.

"Andrea?" He knocked on each container, wanting to shout at the top of his lungs, but keeping his voice normal. "Come on, you've got to be in one of these."

The first rig pulled away, and Pete ran behind the second. If Andrea wasn't inside, he had to stay with the containers in order to find her. He pulled himself on top of the second rig and used the tie-down straps to hold on. He didn't wait long before the second truck slowly bounced across the field, west a few minutes and then south onto Rio Grande Road. The trucks turned toward the border at the railroad.

Above the roar of the wind and road noise, he heard the loud rotation of giant helicopter blades as the trucks came to a halt before the ground dropped away.

He dialed McCrea. "They're at the burned-out rail bridge. There's a heavy-lifting chopper hovering over the water. How fast can you get here?"

"Back off, Pete. We're spread thin on four fronts. We can notify the Mexican authorities to pick them up."

"I'm not leaving. She has to be here." He shoved the phone in his pocket and pulled his weapon. He crawled forward using the cover of the engines to beat on each of the containers, shouting her name, "Andrea!"

"Pete? Pete! It's about time you guys showed up. Let me out of here!"

"It's just me. Pipe down and hold on while I figure out a way to get us out of here."

Men climbed atop the first container, hooking

cables so the helicopter could airlift it over the river. Pete ducked his head, desperately trying to come up with a plan. Before he could free Andrea, he needed keys to the padlock on the door.

Ten guys would come crashing down on him if he fought the big guy shouting orders. He couldn't get close without being recognized as the sheriff. He climbed down the tail end of the truck. Mimicking the smugglers, he tugged at the tie-downs, keeping his face hidden.

Across the river, he saw a train arrive. The chopper stayed low until the last hooks were in place, then took off transporting the first container to the train. At this rate, the exchange wouldn't take long and the smugglers would be out of reach before authorities could track them down.

Pete didn't have much time.

Taking on the leader would only get his head blown off. The solution was dangerous. His timing would have to be perfect and he'd most likely get shot. But he was willing to risk it for Andrea. He couldn't live with himself if he did nothing.

He coiled a tie-down and casually dropped it by the last container. By the time Andrea's was being hooked to the chopper, everything was in place—including himself. The leader gave a thumbs-up to the pilot just as he had for the previous three containers.

Gun in hand, Pete tackled the leader to the ground while everyone was looking up. He threw a punch, connecting the grip of his 9mm with the man's jawbone. Pulling the key ring, he ran to the back of the container. It was a stretch, but he caught the loop he'd tied for a handhold.

Curses. Gunfire. Pings from the ricochets off the steel. He dropped the gun down his T-shirt so he wouldn't lose it while crashing against the side, then pulling himself to the top.

They were flying through the air. Andrea yelled below him, asking what was going on, but there was no time to explain. He slipped his arms through the loop and dropped slowly down in front of the lock. The Rio Grande was below him as he banged around. He finally reached the door, kicking it with his boots to get Andrea's attention.

"Grab hold of something, I'm going to open this thing!"

"Ready."

The lock fell, clanging against the train below. He pushed out from the container. Gravity helped open the door as the chopper got closer to the empty flat car of the train. The darkness helped hide him against the black container. Shots from below. Andrea's smiling face in front of him. Apprehension that he might fail stabbed at his gut.

"Do I pull you inside? Or do you have an escape ladder?" she shouted.

The container was almost in place. A bullet ricocheted too close for comfort. "Steel between us and them might be a good thing." His hand caught the opening, and she caught his waistband.

Once inside, she pulled him close, kissing him before he could get the loop from his body. "So, what's the plan?"

"This is as far as I got."

"Can anyone come to our rescue on this side of the border?" she asked, lifting a handgun, arming it and aiming behind him.

"Not officially. All we have to do is get to the Port of Entry." He pulled the tie-down loop off his body and caught men taking cover behind several vehicles.

"Well, there's plenty of guns and ammo in here." She turned over a tub similar to the one he'd carried to the smugglers. Then she sorted through the smaller boxes in search of the right ammo. "All we need is a getaway car."

"Are you hurt?" He tugged her back into his arms and searched her eyes while she shook her head. "It'll be risky. No brave stunts. You run and you keep running. No matter what happens."

"I promise." She softly touched his split lip, then brought hers to his, clinging for the briefest of moments. Then she darted to the other side of the opening, drawing a couple of shots. "Grab what you need before they shut the door and lock us both in here."

He found ammo, pulled his shirt from his pants and retrieved his weapon. He took another, quickly loading and dropping it in his boot. She was right. If the smugglers were smart, all they had to do was close the door. One thing to their advantage was that the chopper was still attached, so the container was still wobbling around a bit.

"I'll lay down cover while you get to the other side of the train."

"Then I'll do the same for you."

"Look, Andrea. This isn't the same as shooting targets."

"Come on, Pete, we don't have time for lectures. I got this." She placed one gun at the small of her back and had the second ready to fire. "I'll see you in a minute."

He fired. She jumped, rolling out of sight below him. He didn't wait, just reloaded, fired in the direction of movement and followed her.

Backs to a train wheel, Andrea pointed to floodlights from a helicopter hovering on the other side of the river. "Do you think that's my dad? Can we swim across?"

"We can probably walk." He dialed the cell. McCrea answered on the first ring. Pete stated their plans and disconnected. "They agree that it looks like our best way out without your father flying over the river and causing an international incident. Stay low, drop to your belly if you hear anything and don't say a word."

"Got it. But before I stop rambling, thanks for coming to rescue me."

"No problem. It was my—"

"Let's shut up now before you say it was just your job. Go."

She ran. It wasn't far, but it was dangerous. He kept a close eye on the activity behind them. The men at the railroad were no longer worried about the prisoner's escape. They were more worried about their own. Pete followed, knowing that as soon as they crossed that river, he'd lose Andrea for sure.

Chapter Twenty-Seven

Andrea ran. And when her lungs were screaming, she ran some more.

There was very little ground cover, but apparently losing her as a hostage was less important than getting their train out of there quickly. No one followed her and Pete, and in no time at all they were back on U.S. soil. Her father was waiting, hugging her as soon as she sloshed out of the river. Publicly.

"You're not hurt? Thanks to heaven for that. Now your mother won't divorce me," he joked.

Andrea was handed a bottle of water and gulped it down. "What about Sharon?" she finally got out when her dry throat was soothed.

"She was with the men in the truck with the shipment of drugs—if you could really call it a shipment. We stopped it six miles up the road. She looks okay, but drugged so she would cooperate." Her dad squeezed her shoulder, pulling her closer to his side. "We rounded up more than a dozen men at the concert. All in all, I think we can call this a successful operation."

Sharon was okay. She'd helped find her. All the risk had been worth it.

The man who had abducted her on the ATV was lying on his stomach with the rest of the smugglers, hands behind their backs. She felt safe next to her father, but she wanted Pete. She watched him about twenty feet away accepting slaps on the back from his deputies. Their eyes finally met. She gestured for him to come closer. He stayed where he was, his face full of sadness.

"And what about the guy who orchestrated it all?" she asked her dad. "What happened to Mr. Rook?"

"Ranger McCrea radioed that they found him speeding to Alpine and an awaiting private airplane."

"So everything's okay and I can go back to the observatory."

"Absolutely not. We don't know the extent of this operation. You're heading back to Austin with me. In about three minutes. No arguments."

"Yes, sir." She knew Pete heard. His chin dropped to his chest, but he didn't move.

There was so much she wanted to say.

"Pete?" She ran to him, leaving her pride behind. "Come with us," she said, hugging him, not wanting to let him go, wanting to beg him, knowing she wouldn't.

"I can't." He lowered his voice, his breath close

across her ear. "You know why, Andrea." He pulled back, his mouth only a whisper away. "I'm resigning. I can't let my dad's reputation be destroyed."

"But you love being sheriff. I could stay, I don't have to go…"

Pete looked around her to the waiting helicopter and her father. "Yes, you do, darlin', and I have to stay in Marfa. As much as I'd like things to be different, they aren't."

"But I lo —" He covered her lips with a soft touch of his fingers, stopping the words but not the thought. She loved him. Yes, it had only been a week, but she was certain of it. Her heart felt heavenly with the realization, then plummeted with the miserable look on his face.

"Don't say it," he whispered hoarsely. "I couldn't let you go if you said it."

"We can work this out. It doesn't have to be your father or me."

"Dammit. I'm not choosing my dad over you. It's just rotten luck that our fathers are who they are."

"You make us sound like Romeo and Juliet. This can all be worked out. Our families aren't at war. They actually like each other."

"That's just it. You can't lie to your dad. It wouldn't be fair to you. And I can't tell the truth. Not after everything my father did for me. I just can't turn my back on him. If they found him guilty of perjury or forgery, what then? Think of every criminal he's ever put away. They'd appeal their cases. They'd be out of jail faster than a jackrabbit back in its hole."

"I understand, but there has to be a better solution than never seeing each other again."

"Andrea, it's time," her father called behind her.

She wrapped her arm around Pete's neck and gave a little tug. He came closer—a willing partner, knowing her intention. He meant their kiss to be a goodbye. She couldn't stand that it was. Hot, hurried, desperate. Their bodies molded together. She didn't want to let him go.

She couldn't let him go.

"Please don't cry, Andrea," he said against her lips, wiping a tear that had fallen to her cheek. "You've got to go. He's waiting." He reached up, holding her hands as they slid across his chest.

She already ached to touch his warm skin and play with the hair falling across his forehead. She turned and ran, afraid to look back at him. She'd scream how wrong he had to be. Or she'd shout over the whirling blades that she loved him. Then everyone would know she'd been rejected, that he was letting her go, practically chasing her away.

The door of the chopper closed, and they lifted off.

"I was thinking about offering Pete Morrison a job," her father said without the benefit of the headset and microphone. No one else could hear their conversation. "Funny thing. Pete Morrison doesn't exist on paper. At least not the man you just desperately kissed goodbye."

"And you didn't arrest him?"

"I'm assuming there's a logical explanation. I don't know the particulars yet. Do you?" He smiled. Totally her father. The Commander was nowhere in sight. He could tell Pete was a good man.

"Dad, I have a huge favor to ask you as soon as we get back."

Chapter Twenty-Eight

It was a night just like all the rest before Pete had met Andrea. He was in his service vehicle driving Highway 90. Everything was quiet. Too quiet. The quieter it was, the more he thought about the mistake he'd made letting Andrea go.

Would he be destined to live on the ranch alone like his dad? Keeping secrets, scraping together enough to keep a few head of cattle.

His father was angry with him and as a result so were Peach and Honey. His family. And they were all disappointed that he'd let Andrea leave and hadn't called her in the week since.

There wasn't another way round it. He couldn't ask her to live a lie with him. It was his burden to bear.

"That sounds so stupid. Just get a grip on yourself. It wasn't a mistake. You were protecting her." He hit the steering wheel, leaving the palm of his hand stinging.

"Sheriff?" Honey's voice came through the radio.

"Yes, ma'am."

"We have a report of unusual activity at the Viewing Area. Do you think the smugglers are back?"

"I'm heading there now. Out."

He was only a couple of miles away. Heading east, he couldn't see if the Marfa lights were visible behind him. There wasn't anything to the south—at least not in his line of sight. He slowed his approach.

There was one car in the lot, one person standing on the platform. Tight jeans hugging a figure he remembered all too well.

Andrea?

That was wishful thinking. Her father would never let her set foot in this town again. He got out of the car, not mentioning to Honey that he'd arrived. His feet wanted to run and spin the woman around to verify what his heart told him. It was her. It had to be.

And in that moment he knew beyond a doubt that he couldn't stay away from her. He loved Andrea Allen. Sure, they needed to learn more about each other, but this was different than anything he'd experienced. And he wanted more.

"Did you call for assistance, miss?"

"No. Honey thought it would get you here faster." Andrea turned, leaning on the railing with a large envelope in her hand.

"What are you doing— Should you— Why are you here?" he stammered.

"I need to ask you a question."

"Right here? Couldn't you just ask on the phone?"

"No. I needed to see your face. But out here in only starlight might not have been such a good idea." She slid her fingers around the edge of the envelope, nervously touching every side as it rotated in her hands.

"What's your question?"

"To answer your second question, I didn't want an audience when I asked. Or when I gave you this."

"What's in the envelope?"

"First, my question. Do you like me?"

"Of course. Is there more?"

"Do you like me enough to give whatever's between us a shot? I mean, if you're not forcing me to lie to my father. That was the only reason you gave, but it could have just been an easy way out for you."

"There was nothing easy about letting you get on that helicopter." Protective emotions slammed him. She shouldn't be anywhere close to Marfa and yet he couldn't let her go. Not again.

She sighed and turned to face the mountains. He didn't analyze his actions. He simply walked to her and dropped his arms around her waist, pulling her into the curve of his body. He wanted to spin her around and kiss her into oblivion, but that's where he stopped. She'd come a long way to say whatever she was trying to say.

"I could get used to this." She linked her fingers with his and rested her head on his shoulder.

He could, too.

"I thought the only thing I wanted was to make my own discovery. A distant star that no one had ever seen before. Then I came here. With all the stars up there to see every night, I ran out of reasons to find another." She twisted in his arms, staying close, then skimmed her fingers through his hair, ending at the back of his neck. The envelope stayed in her left hand, dangling behind his back.

"I missed you. Missed the conversations that I didn't totally understand. Missed smelling your shampoo and soap when the steam from your bathroom found its way into the hall. Everything you feel about stars…I feel about you. I—" He was choking up, but had to tell her. It might be his only chance, and she deserved the truth. "If things were different, I wouldn't let you go. I've never felt this way about anyone, Andrea."

He leaned in to kiss her, but his lips found her neck instead.

She tilted her head enough to meet his eyes. "I feel the same and I'm so happy. I think you should know that I accepted a job."

Gut kicked. Stomped by a bronc. The pain shooting through him was worse. His lonely life passed before his eyes. He'd looked up just how far away those jobs were. They might as well be on one of those stars she studied, since he couldn't follow her.

"I'm not sure I understand. Why'd you risk coming here to tell me you'll be living halfway round the world?"

"It's actually not that far." Her voice had the twinkle in it that made his mouth curl in a smile.

But not today. He didn't have the patience for teasing. He gently set her away from him and saw the laughter in her eyes. "Just where is this job?"

"At the observatory. I never thought I'd enjoy teaching, but I love it. Love the kids and all their questions. The stargazing parties turned me on to a new way of seeing the sky."

"But that means—"

"That we can work on this chemistry we seem to have?" She tapped the envelope against her thigh.

"What's inside?"

"Well, turns out my father knew about your false identity."

His mind exploded, running every scenario through his brain at once. What would happen to his dad?

"Before you go off the deep end. After a conversation with Joe, my dad used some connections and fixed everything." She handed him the envelope. "Meet Pete Morrison. Passport, birth certificate, adoption papers. Don't be mad at your dad for keeping it a secret. I asked to be the one to tell you."

"I don't know what to say. I never thought…"

"I know. When I asked him, I didn't think he could manage all this. I thought he might smooth things over, keep it out of the courts. But he does know some influential people who obviously believed in you both. You're completely legit, Sheriff." She pressed the envelope to his chest.

"Come here." Capturing her lips under his reemphasized just what a fool he'd been. No other woman would ever take Andrea's place. She was his, but more important, he belonged with her.

"There is one little catch my dad insisted on," she whispered.

"Whatever he wants," he whispered back, "we'll manage. I'm not letting you go again."

"Good, because he's insisting I stay at your place and act as if I'm under house arrest until your task force is finished."

"That's not a favor, it's a reward." He kissed her again to seal the deal. "Are you sure you'll be satisfied looking at the stars from West Texas?"

"As long as I look at them occasionally with the man I love...I'll be more than happy."

* * * * *

Don't miss the next book in Angi Morgan's miniseries, WEST TEXAS WATCHMEN, *when* THE CATTLEMAN *goes on sale next month. You'll find it wherever Harlequin Intrigue books are sold!*

LARGER-PRINT
BOOKS!

LARGER-PRINT BOOKS!

GET 2 FREE LARGER-PRINT NOVELS PLUS
2 FREE GIFTS!

HARLEQUIN®

Romance

From the Heart, For the Heart

YES! Please send me 2 FREE LARGER-PRINT Harlequin® Romance novels and my 2 FREE gifts (gifts are worth about $10). After receiving them, if I don't wish to receive any more books, I can return the shipping statement marked "cancel." If I don't cancel, I will receive 4 brand-new novels every month and be billed just $4.84 per book in the U.S. or $5.24 per book in Canada. That's a savings of at least 19% off the cover price! It's quite a bargain! Shipping and handling is just 50¢ per book in the U.S. and 75¢ per book in Canada.* I understand that accepting the 2 free books and gifts places me under no obligation to buy anything. I can always return a shipment and cancel at any time. Even if I never buy another book, the two free books and gifts are mine to keep forever.

119/319 HDN F43Y

Name _____ (PLEASE PRINT)

Address _____ Apt. #

City _____ State/Prov. _____ Zip/Postal Code

Signature (if under 18, a parent or guardian must sign)

Mail to the **Harlequin® Reader Service:**
IN U.S.A.: P.O. Box 1867, Buffalo, NY 14240-1867
IN CANADA: P.O. Box 609, Fort Erie, Ontario L2A 5X3
Want to try two free books from another line?
Call 1-800-873-8635 or visit www.ReaderService.com.

* Terms and prices subject to change without notice. Prices do not include applicable taxes. Sales tax applicable in N.Y. Canadian residents will be charged applicable taxes. Offer not valid in Quebec. This offer is limited to one order per household. Not valid for current subscribers to Harlequin Romance Larger-Print books. All orders subject to credit approval. Credit or debit balances in a customer's account(s) may be offset by any other outstanding balance owed by or to the customer. Please allow 4 to 6 weeks for delivery. Offer available while quantities last.

Your Privacy—The Harlequin® Reader Service is committed to protecting your privacy. Our Privacy Policy is available online at www.ReaderService.com or upon request from the Harlequin Reader Service.

We make a portion of our mailing list available to reputable third parties that offer products we believe may interest you. If you prefer that we not exchange your name with third parties, or if you wish to clarify or modify your communication preferences, please visit us at www.ReaderService.com/consumerschoice or write to us at Harlequin Reader Service Preference Service, P.O. Box 9062, Buffalo, NY 14269. Include your complete name and address.

HRLP13R

LARGER-PRINT BOOKS!
GET 2 FREE LARGER-PRINT NOVELS PLUS
2 FREE GIFTS!

HARLEQUIN
super romance

More Story...More Romance

YES! Please send me 2 FREE LARGER-PRINT Harlequin® Superromance® novels and my 2 FREE gifts (gifts are worth about $10). After receiving them, if I don't wish to receive any more books, I can return the shipping statement marked "cancel." If I don't cancel, I will receive 6 brand-new novels every month and be billed just $5.69 per book in the U.S. or $5.99 per book in Canada. That's a savings of at least 16% off the cover price! It's quite a bargain! Shipping and handling is just 50¢ per book in the U.S. or 75¢ per book in Canada.* I understand that accepting the 2 free books and gifts places me under no obligation to buy anything. I can always return a shipment and cancel at any time. Even if I never buy another book, the two free books and gifts are mine to keep forever.

139/339 HDN F46Y

Name	(PLEASE PRINT)

Address	Apt. #

City	State/Prov.	Zip/Postal Code

Signature (if under 18, a parent or guardian must sign)

Mail to the **Harlequin® Reader Service:**
IN U.S.A.: P.O. Box 1867, Buffalo, NY 14240-1867
IN CANADA: P.O. Box 609, Fort Erie, Ontario L2A 5X3

Are you a current subscriber to Harlequin Superromance books and want to receive the larger-print edition?
Call 1-800-873-8635 today or visit www.ReaderService.com.

* Terms and prices subject to change without notice. Prices do not include applicable taxes. Sales tax applicable in N.Y. Canadian residents will be charged applicable taxes. Offer not valid in Quebec. This offer is limited to one order per household. Not valid for current subscribers to Harlequin Superromance Larger-Print books. All orders subject to credit approval. Credit or debit balances in a customer's account(s) may be offset by any other outstanding balance owed by or to the customer. Please allow 4 to 6 weeks for delivery. Offer available while quantities last.

Your Privacy—The Harlequin® Reader Service is committed to protecting your privacy. Our Privacy Policy is available online at www.ReaderService.com or upon request from the Harlequin Reader Service.

We make a portion of our mailing list available to reputable third parties that offer products we believe may interest you. If you prefer that we not exchange your name with third parties, or if you wish to clarify or modify your communication preferences, please visit us at www.ReaderService.com/consumerschoice or write to us at Harlequin Reader Service Preference Service, P.O. Box 9062, Buffalo, NY 14269. Include your complete name and address.

HSRLP13R